MELON HEAD
MAYHEM

ALEX EBENSTEIN

MELON HEAD MAYHEM

KILLER VHS SERIES
BOOK 1

SHORTWAVE
PUBLISHING

Copyright © 2023 by Alex Ebenstein

Cover design by Marc Vuletich and Alan Lastufka.
Interior design by Alan Lastufka.

First Edition published July 2023.

10 9 8 7 6 5 4 3 2 1

ISBN 978-1-959565-15-4 (Paperback)
ISBN 978-1-959565-16-1 (eBook)

For my boy, who helps me remember the joy in imagination.

CHAPTER ONE

The '80s horror VHS was in the back of his dead grandmother's closet. Carson found the tape buried beneath a mountain of old shoes on his third attempt to clean out the room. On the cover was a shaggy gray creature with claws on each hand and foot, and a devilish grin chock full of tiny, jagged teeth. The red text in prototypical futuristic font across the bottom read "CRITTERS."

It was one of the few horror movies from that era he hadn't seen, and he reckoned it would be a good distraction from the past few days' events. . . but where to find a VCR?

Carson pulled out his phone and called his cousin, Sophia.

"Hey, Carson. Decided you wanted to take me up on the offer to help clean Gran's place after all?"

"Actually, no. I'm hoping you can do me one better. Does your dad still have a VCR laying around?"

Sophia had driven across the state for Gran's funeral and was staying at her childhood home for the week. Wanting to be around to help, wanting to be there for her dad, Carson's uncle. Carson was glad to hear of her plans, not only because the three of them were the only family left to handle the proceedings, but because he missed spending time with her.

She sighed, embarrassed. "You know he does."

"Perfect." Carson smiled to himself. "Because, shockingly, despite all the crap in this house, the one thing Gran didn't have was a VCR. Can I borrow it?"

"What do you want that for? Are you feeling all right?"

Carson clicked his tongue. "Yes, I'm fine, Soph. Do you remember Isaac, from high school? And that big box of horror VHS tapes from the video store? I found a leftover in Gran's closet."

"Oh yeah? Which one?"

"*Critters*. I've never seen it before. Thought it might be a fun distraction."

"That's a good one. You'll like it." She paused. "Mind if I watch it with you? I could use a break. I'm sure my dad could too. I can bring the VCR over right now...?"

"Of course! Goes without saying Rae's welcome too."

"She drove back home to the east side already. She only had time for the funeral. Back to work now, as usual... I'm still staying the rest of the week, though."

Secretly he felt relief. He liked Sophia's wife, a lot even, but it had been far too long since he and Sophia had a chance to hang out one on one. Yet, there was something in Sophia's voice...

"Everything good with Rae?" Neither he nor Sophia were ones for tiptoeing around difficult conversations. Directness was a key to their closeness—even throughout the years of Carson drifting around the country—and he'd be damned if he changed that now. If she didn't like the bluntness, she'd say so.

"No 'trouble.' Rae's great. We're great."

"But?"

"But. . . But nothing. It's not important, and certainly not as important as me coming over right now to watch a silly horror movie."

Before he could respond, she added, "Be there in ten," and hung up.

While Carson waited for Sophia, he thought back to that once magnificent collection of horror flicks. He'd gotten them from his buddy, Isaac, who worked at Movie Gallery until the beloved video rental store finally went out of business. Carson, who was a young teen at the time, had thus far been deprived of mature movies, especially horror—so he was thrilled to get a treasure trove. But he ended up owning the boxes of tapes for less than a week. Gran confiscated them the second she laid eyes on the movie covers lining the top row. Equal parts gruesome and salacious, they were almost enough to still Gran's good Christian heart. And if Carson was being honest with himself, those covers often made him feel like he was sneaking a peek at something he was far too young to be seeing. The cover for *The Slumber Party Massacre*, in particular, was burned into his puberty-rattled brain.

Having them taken away, Carson was furious as only a teen could be—but that anger quickly dissipated once he discovered Sophia's dad had salvaged them from the trash bin. Uncle Dave was a big movie guy and had a great fondness for horror, which he passed on to his daughter and nephew. Carson knew he could watch the movies at their house anytime.

He looked at the movie in his hand again, the cover rather tame compared to most of the others he remembered. He popped open the hard plastic case to get a look at the obsolete video tech, but frowned when he saw what was inside. It *was* a VHS tape, but it was one of those blanks you'd record on at home, not a video store rental.

Carson took the tape out of the case and found the words *Revenge of the Melon Heads! (1986)* inscribed in pencil on the white sticker label along the edge. Melon Heads sounded sort of familiar, but he didn't think he'd heard of the film before. Even though the 1980s were before his time, Carson now fancied himself a bit of an aficionado, having watched all those rental tapes and catching up on the deep cuts via streaming since then— so it was surprising to not even recognize this one. *Revenge of the Melon Heads!* had to be horror with a title like that and screamed low budget. Maybe even homemade.

So much for Critters, he thought. *Well, maybe this will be better.*

Sophia arrived a few minutes later and entered cautiously, her wary expression implying the same feeling Carson had been fighting since he got to town a few days earlier: the house simply felt wrong without Gran in it. The frequent clatter of dishes in the kitchen while she wreaked havoc attempting to bake, or the lilting, off-tune snippets of made-up songs—all gone. The often overpowering scent of lavender had already begun to fade.

Carson gave Sophia a careful, knowing smile, an acknowledgment. She nodded with a slanted smile of her own, then followed him into the living room. As she set the VCR down next to the TV, he filled her in on his discovery, showing her the rewritable tape, label out.

"Do you know anything about it?" she asked.

"Never heard of it," Carson replied, shaking his head. "I'm guessing it's terrible. But, maybe it's one of those 'so bad it's kind of good' movies, you know? Ooh, maybe it'll be like *Killer Klowns from Outer Space*! God, I love that awful movie."

Sophia laughed. "Funny enough, I saw *Killer Klowns* in my dad's basement den while grabbing the VCR."

"No kidding? Does your dad still have all the old tapes?"

"Of course he does. They're all on display too, practically a damn shrine to the 'golden age of horror,' or whatever dumb thing he likes to say."

Carson whistled. "Man, your dad is so cool."

"No, my dad is a massive nerd, just like you."

"Ouch, shots fired! That hurts, Soph," he said, but was laughing too. "So, we doing this or what? Want to see what these melon head things are all about?"

"Hey, I'm still game to watch it if you are."

CHAPTER TWO

"Wait, how do we know this doesn't have some homemade sex tape on it?" Sophia asked. "I miss Gran, but I think I'd be scarred for life if that's what this was."

Carson had the VCR hooked up to the TV and was about to insert the tape. "Ugh, gross. What is wrong with you?"

"Well, it *could* be. We don't know."

"You and I both know it's not. Come on. Gran and Gramps? No chance."

"You found it in a rental case, right? It could have come from anywhere."

Carson frowned. "You're right. But we won't know for sure unless we watch it. Do you want to or not?"

She laughed. "Of course, I do. I'm just messing with you. Now let's go!"

Carson pushed the tape in and bounced back to the couch. Sophia passed him the bowl of popcorn she'd made. For a second, nostalgia choked him up. This moment, settled into the couch, excited to watch a movie and eating popcorn. . . it was all exactly the same as he remembered when they were kids. An only child, Carson had been taken in by his grandparents after his mom died in a car wreck. Sophia—a similar age—lived nearby, so they hung out all the time, mostly to watch movies. Those were some of the only happy moments in Carson's life at that time. Mirrored now in the wake of Gran's passing, a fragment of happiness.

Sophia gave him her patented one-sided smile and he knew she felt it too. Right now, things were good.

Carson pressed 'Play' on the remote. The black TV screen blipped with streaks of white static and flashes of distorted color before morphing into a scene of crashing waves on a sandy shoreline. There was no way to tell if this was the beginning of the movie since there were no opening credits or titles, but it appeared that way.

The camera panned up from the waves revealing large sand dunes and, eventually, a towering Victorian mansion perched on the horizon. . .

Cut to the main characters—thus initiating Carson and Sophia's running commentary over the movie, because they simply couldn't help it.

"Here's *Randy*, our *totally rad dude* with the mullet and red convertible," Carson said.

"Don't forget Jenny, the pretty blonde coed girl-friend," Sophia countered. "Wouldn't do to have a plain Jane girlfriend for *Randy*."

The couple were on summer break from college, working part-time jobs at the mansion—Barton Mansion—a newly renovated inn. Not long after they started working there, the two were approached by a man on the outskirts of the grounds.

"Ahh yes, *the creepy local*, complete with long, stringy hair and a fistful of missing teeth," Carson said.

"Let me guess. He's going to tell them Barton Mansion is haunted. He's going to issue the *dire warning*," Sophia said.

Not haunted, but she was close.

According to *the creepy local*, before the bed and breakfast, Barton Mansion was abandoned. And before that, it was owned by eccentric millionaire and self-proclaimed scientist, Harold Barton, who also ran a sort of insane asylum at the far end of his property. In the asylum, Barton performed highly unethical experiments on children in an attempt to produce superhuman intelligence. He created monsters instead. Devilish humanoids called "melon heads" that promptly exacted their revenge and killed Barton. This all happened back in the 1930s, and while the asylum has since been leveled, the creepy old man assured Randy and Jenny that the melon heads still lived on the grounds, terrorizing anyone who encroached on their territory.

"Okay, so we've got bulbous-headed, bloodthirsty monsters with super strength and an insatiable thirst for revenge," Carson said. "Oh, and they basically live forever."

"Solid premise, I'd say," Sophia said.

They watched as Jenny and Randy laughed at the spooky tale, ridiculed the old man, and wrote off the whole mess as a nonsense urban legend. That was, until some of their coworkers started to vanish. . .

"And cue the bloodshed," Carson said.

Moments later, onscreen, one of the missing coworkers was found. Unfortunately for the coworker, she was in pieces, limbs and torso spread across the grounds in front of the mansion, the lawn soaked red.

Naturally, mayhem ensued.

"Well, it's up to Jenny and Randy now, isn't it? Who else will find a way to stop the melon heads?" Sophia said.

The next thirty minutes consisted of not much more than Randy and Jenny running for their lives, as well as a slew of tertiary character deaths. At one point, inexplicably, the two stopped running in order to sneak into a vacant room and have sex.

"*Whelp*, here it is. I wondered when this would happen," Sophia said, standing. "I'm going to go grab some more popcorn. Enjoy those '80s boobs."

Carson laughed. "You know how it is. Can't figure out where the plot's going? Just add nudity. The shitty horror movie fix-all."

Sophia waved a hand at him and went off to the kitchen. When she returned five minutes later she said, "What did I miss?"

"Not much. That sex scene lasted much longer than I expected, then there was some more unnecessary, but glorious gore, and now Jenny and Randy are in the basement. Where it looks like they just might find. . ."

"Oh! A secret room!" Sophia shouted, plopping back onto the couch.

The secret room was Harold's old study, full of dust and cobwebs and a miraculously intact office setup. In a locked desk drawer—that easily succumbed to Randy's macho strength—they found Harold's personal journal. The journal contained everything Jenny and Randy would hope to know about the ill-advised experiments, and then some. Including the one foolproof method of killing the melon heads.

"Okay, so they know how to kill the monsters. A little too convenient, but I'll accept it."

"I mean, it's fine. But why wasn't Harold able to take care of his own mess? They were his monsters, after all."

They never did find out, but Jenny and Randy were able to use this secret weapon to dispose of the melon heads one by one. Eventually, they arrived at the *final showdown*. The confrontation started in the woods surrounding the mansion and ended up on the sandy beach of the lake. In a heroic, yet entirely stupid move—

"Don't do it, Randy. Don't do it," Carson said.

"Do it! Do it! Do it!" Sophia chanted.

—Randy threw himself in front of an attacking monster, sufficiently sacrificing himself to save *his girl*. Jenny, grief-stricken, but thankfully not *hysterical*, as '80s horror movie women are wont to be, easily killed the last melon head, who was preoccupied with feeding on the now-dead Randy.

The movie ended with Jenny slumped on the sand, crying, as bloody, bubbly water surged around her.

The video cut to static.

"And so," Carson said, "survival was attained."

"But at what cost?" Sophia asked.

Carson pointed at his cousin in acknowledgement

and agreement. They both laughed and shook their heads.

"Man," Carson said. "That was. . . terrible. But also, kind of awesome."

"Hey, the chick survived at least, so that must count for something," Sophia said, standing. She went to the VCR, reached for the 'Eject' button.

"Hey!" Carson yelled.

Sophia jumped, almost knocking the VCR off the shelf. She turned to Carson, glaring. "Dude, what gives?"

Carson grinned. "Be kind. Rewind."

They both burst out laughing. It really wasn't funny at all, but it was so typical of their old humor that with everything else going on, the nostalgic vibes, it happened to be the perfect joke for the situation. It left them in the kind of laughter that would have ended in tears had it not been for the new noise coming from the TV.

The static had suddenly given way to a close-up shot of a disheveled man's face, his hair in disarray and his thick-framed glasses practically diagonal across his filthy face. Sweat and dirt and. . . was that blood? The video quality made it hard to tell, but it looked like the man had several scratches on his cheeks and nose. The man was whispering hurriedly into the camera while repeatedly looking back over his shoulder.

"I don't know who will see this, but it's real. It's *all* real. It's not supposed to be, but it is. We all thought we were just making a silly film about an urban legend. I mean, God, we were! The film isn't real, but, like, somehow our production. . . summoned them? Like it brought them to life or something. I know, I know. That sounds crazy. But it's true. We think they really do want revenge. Or maybe they feel threatened by the film." The man's voice faltered, a sob came in its place. "Oh God, I don't think we'll survive the night."

Static.

CHAPTER THREE

"What the fuck?"

"It's a joke. Right?" Sophia said with no certainty. "I mean, it has to be. *Melon heads* aren't *real*." Slightly more confident, but not much.

"Right, got to be a prank," Carson asserted, but his thumbnail rubbing against his bottom lip contradicted the sentiment. It was a tic-like behavior, a relic from his now broken habit of biting his nails, though was not one of pure nervousness—more an indication of his brain trying to make sense of something.

Sophia returned to the couch without shutting off the VCR.

"Who was that guy?" she asked.

"No clue."

"Do you know anything about the movie? About who made it?"

"Honestly, no. Thought about checking Google but never did."

Sophia swiped at her phone for a minute. "Hmm, okay. Well, I might have something. . . Did melon heads sound familiar to you?"

"Vaguely, sure."

"Right, me too. The legend of the melon heads exists in a few places, and one of those is right here in West Michigan."

Carson's eyes widened. "Oh duh, that's right! I remember hearing about that when we were kids. They were said to be out in the woods along Lake Michigan. Over by..."

Carson and Sophia locked eyes and finished the sentence at the same time. "Felt Mansion."

"No wonder this seemed oddly familiar. Barton Mansion is supposed to be Felt Mansion."

"Yep," Sophia said, nodding her head. "Jesus, only thirty minutes from here."

She bent back to her phone, tapping away. "No shit..."

"What? What is it?"

"I found something a few pages deep," she said, then started mumbling to herself, reading intermittently out loud.

"... reported filming at Felt Mansion... something about an urban legend... crew missing... director, Ryan —Oh, wow. It's him!"

"What? Who?"

Sophia grabbed the remote from the couch cushion between them and rewound the tape. When she got back to the guy, she paused the tape, freezing the man's distorted and bloody face on the TV. Then she showed Carson her phone screen.

"It's him," she said, pointing at the TV. "Ryan A. Henderson. Writer slash director slash producer. I think he made this movie. But. . ."

"But what?" Carson asked.

"But he disappeared. Back in the '80s. No one ever found him. There were rumors he was shooting a secret movie out at Felt Mansion. I'm not sure they had permission. . ." Sophia looked up at Carson. "And then he vanished. Him and his whole crew."

"Come on, really? That's impossible. The whole crew up and vanished without a trace?"

"That's what this article says, but who knows." She was looking at the TV again, the haunted, attacked face of Ryan Henderson. "This is weird, though, right?"

"Very weird." He was on his phone now, too, looking at the image results of his melon head search. "It's interesting, there aren't many pictures of what these monsters look like."

"You mean the non-existent creatures? Yeah, no shit, Sherlock."

"You know what I mean," Carson said, rolling his eyes at her. "You search the internet for Mothman or the Jersey Devil and you get hundreds of drawings and renderings. For being a multi-state legend, there's not a whole lot of info on them."

"That's probably why that dude made a movie about them. Hard for people to complain about the costume design when there's nothing to compare to."

"Although, they did look cheesy as hell," Carson said.

Sophia laughed briefly, then gestured at the TV. "Do we need to do something about this?"

"Nah, I don't think so. It all happened thirty-plus

years ago, yeah? So even if it *was* something—" He tossed his hands in the air. "—it's nothing now."

"True." She stood, stretched, and gave an exaggerated yawn. "Well, I'm tired. Mr. Henderson there would have to wait until tomorrow anyway. Actually, do you mind if I take the tape? Not much going on at the house tomorrow. I think my dad would get a kick out of it, maybe help cheer him up."

Carson shrugged. "Go for it. I've seen it enough for one lifetime."

She ejected the tape, tossed it in her bag, and started for the door. Halfway, she stopped, holding up a finger, then retraced her steps to the VCR, unhooked it, and pulled it under her arm. Carson laughed, understanding. Even with the old, physical media in hand, their brains had been so heavily trained to think *digital* or *streaming media* first.

"Thanks for giving me a call, Car. That was fun. And, remember, I'm around all week. Let me know if I can help you out around here.

CHAPTER FOUR

The doorbell jostled Carson awake. He meant to do some more cleaning after Sophia left, but he made the mistake of lying down on the couch and dozed off almost instantly; a fitful sleep full of bizarro dreams and nightmares, melon heads and mansions.

Carson opened the front door.

A figure in a brown trench coat, wide-brimmed top hat. Possibly a man, but hard to tell with the mostly shadowed face. At once Carson noticed the odd proportions. Broad midsection, narrow shoulders, extra-large head...

The figure tilted its head up, revealing a smiling row of sharp, pointed teeth. A shark's grin. Fiery amber eyes blazed through the shadow cast by the hat.

Carson felt the danger before he knew it, stumbled back into the house.

The figure ripped away the trench coat. Two humanoid children remained, one standing upon the narrow shoulders of the other. Their bodies were ghastly thin, but wiry. Their heads enormous.

Carson opened his mouth to scream as they both lunged—

He woke for real, his lips forming an *O*, a scream stuck in his throat. He gasped once to catch the breath he'd been holding. His shirt stuck to him, plastered to his body by sweat. He wanted to laugh it off, ridicule himself for allowing a cheap, cheesy horror movie get to him, but he couldn't. He couldn't shake the feeling he got from that last nightmare, as absurd as it was.

His phone told him it was only three-thirty in the morning, but he got up anyway, barely entertaining the thought of going back to bed in the guest room where he'd been sleeping since he got to town. Instead, he started a pot of coffee and tried cleaning again. Anything to get him moving, be productive. Regardless of his and its future, the place needed to be organized and cleaned, all of Gran's things donated or thrown away. He couldn't put it off any longer. Carson knew he'd eventually have to make his way into his old room too. Though at this point he wasn't sure if his avoidance was rooted in the potentially painful memories he might find, or the realization that he was an idiot for leaving it, and his grandparents, the way he had a decade earlier.

As he poured himself a mug of coffee, his phone chirped. Sophia.

Hey Car, you awake?

Yeah. . . don't tell me. Nightmares?

Yep. Mind if I come back over? I can't convince myself to go back to sleep and want something to do. I'll help you clean.

Coffee's ready.

Carson set his phone down next to his laptop on the

island counter and felt the pull to boot up the machine and get some work done while he waited for his cousin. He even placed a hand on the computer, briefly, before pulling it back as if slapped, or scolded.

No. No work. His company had bereavement leave and he intended to use it. Just because he *could* do his work from anywhere, thanks to his laptop, didn't mean he *should*. Especially not right now. If work needed to be done, then his boss could figure out how to get it done without him. He was a web designer, not a brain surgeon.

He wasn't here to work, period. He was back at his longest tenured childhood home to grieve, and to make sense of what was left. And, perhaps, to decide if this is where he wanted to stay. A big part of him did want to stay and settle. The promise of stability and family and—hell, maybe even a more traditional nine-to-five; some job he could leave behind at the end of each workday so he could live his life outside of it, enjoy a hobby or find a partner or...

What was the saying? *Work to live, not live to work.*

There were obvious benefits to sticking around town, Carson knew. But he couldn't deny that it was tough to be here and remember back to his childhood—when he allowed himself to go beyond the surface memories of good times with Sophia or his few high school friends like Isaac. He was a stubborn, angry, and disrespectful boy, and his grandparents took the brunt of these emotions. But did they ever turn their backs on him? Of course not. They let him know when he was being a brat, yet never stopped caring or providing for him. He owed them his life, and what did he do in return? Hit the road the first chance he had with hardly a glance back in the following ten years.

He looked around the kitchen now, one of the few rooms largely cleaned up, imagining the chaos it often held in the wake of Gran's personal whirlwind. She loved this room more than any of the others, loved to cook and bake—with varying success—because it was a way she could be creative. Teenage Carson spent as little time in here as he could, not accepting the constant, but supposedly controlled mess, and not appreciating the art of failure. Current Carson cursed his younger self for missing opportunities to learn some valuable lessons, not to mention spending quality time with Gran.

Maybe he really could fill this room, this house, with a whirlwind of his own, settling down for the first time since moving away. He could learn to cook from Gran's recipes, learn to survive without relying on takeout.

Maybe he could make up for his actions, if only to prove to himself he could. . .

Carson brought the coffee to his lips when a loud bang at the front door nearly knocked the mug out of his hands, splashing hot liquid everywhere.

"Carson! Let me in!"

Carson stood, wiping his hands on the table cloth, muttering. "Sheesh, she's impatient."

Bang. Bang.

"CARSON, HURRY!"

He froze. That was not impatience. That was a scream. A tone of terror. Carson ran to the door, scrambled with the deadbolt, yanked the door open. Sophia leaped through the opening, knocking Carson back.

"Close the door!" she shrieked. "Quick! Quick!"

He hesitated. "What is—"

"NOW!!"

He slammed the door and snapped the lock shut. "Sophia, what is going on?"

She wasn't listening anymore. She shrugged her bag off her shoulder onto the floor then set about looking around. Looking for something.

"Sophia!" Finally getting her attention. "What are you doing?"

"Looking for a weapon," she said quickly. "Did Gran have a gun?"

"A gun? What? Why?" He watched her body tremble once more, then an air of remarkable resolve settled in across her face.

"They're here."

There was no further explanation. Sophia was off, racing around the house checking the lock on the back door and every window. Soon she was moving furniture to create barricades. Carson repeatedly asked her who, exactly, was here. She didn't answer. But really, he already knew. He just didn't want to believe it.

Eventually Sophia rejoined him in the living room with a wooden baseball bat taken from Carson's old bedroom. It was a gift from his grandfather shortly after Carson came to stay for good, autographed by someone Carson didn't know—sports weren't really his thing, not that he ever told Gramps. Sophia scanned the room around her once more for good measure. She looked satisfied and even more calm, if not at ease, having been proactive against whatever this was that was going on.

Finally, she turned to him, raising the bat. "Is this all you have?"

"All I have for what?"

"A weapon. Duh. The melon heads—they're real, and they're here."

So, there it was. Exactly what he expected, yet astonishingly unbelievable.

When he spoke, he tried to reason—whether with Sophia or his own disbelief, he wasn't sure. "You saw them?"

"Yes."

"In your dreams. Right?"

Sophia sighed. "Can we go ahead and skip the part where you kind of definitely think I'm crazy and you need me to prove it? This isn't a movie. This is real life. Besides, we know each other better than that, right? The melon heads are *real*, Carson. And they tried to attack me when I went out to my car. That director guy, Ryan whatever—he was telling the truth. They're after us."

Carson needed a moment for his brain to process the impossible.

"I have so many questions," he said. "Like, why—"

"We don't have time for questions. They'll probably be here any—"

Bang.

The front door again. Then a second later a thud, this time from the back of the house. Immediately after came a screeching, spine-grating scratch across the curtained window behind Carson.

He flipped around in every direction, looking for the source of the noises surrounding them.

"How many are there?" he whispered.

"I don't know. I saw two, but I guess there could have been three."

The assaults continued, coming faster now, but still sounding like the monsters were on the outside of the house. Carson felt stuck in place. He'd never felt fear like this before, never expected it would be so paralyzing.

Thank God Sophia was there.

"We have to be prepared for the likelihood that they get in. Grab a weapon. A knife, something to swing at them with. Anything. Come on, Car. Get moving."

And he did.

He raced into the kitchen—Sophia tailing close behind—and grabbed the biggest knife from the block, a lengthy carving knife complete with small serrations along the cutting edge. He held it up to Sophia to examine. She nodded and grinned, and it hit him that she was starting to enjoy this. She looked like she felt confident and ready to take on some horror movie monsters, and that scared the hell out of Carson. But he also felt in awe of his cousin right then. He always knew she was a badass, but this took the cake.

"So now what?" he asked.

T he first one got in through a back window. Shattered, from the sounds of it. Carson and Sophia stood back to back in the hallway, waiting for this moment that didn't take long to come. Carson had barely enough time to call 9-1-1, which was no help anyway because he made the mistake of telling the truth. The operator didn't remotely believe him, and when Carson tried to take it back and offer the generic *someone is breaking into my home,* he received a healthy scolding and was told not to waste the emergency responders' time. No amount of pleading and protest could prevent the operator hanging up.

They were alone to fight the monsters, one of which was now emerging from the back bedroom at the end of the hallway, pausing to face Sophia, sizing her up.

Carson caught a glimpse over her shoulder, saw the bulbous head, rows of dagger teeth, pale slender frame that appeared scaly. It was a melon head as seen on the movie, to a *T.* Even so far as bearing the hallmarks of the cheesy, unrealistic costumes and animated graphics of an '80s movie. Carson may have been able to convince himself it was all a dream had the melon head not suddenly charged them.

Sophia bumped Carson back as she squared up with the bat.

The monster moved so fast. Carson watched, wanting to help, but couldn't make himself. Sophia stood her ground, ready.

The monster launched itself at Sophia and she swung. The bat connected with the monster's head with a hollow *thunk*, but the impact was minimal. Sophia managed to deflect some of the attack, but not enough to avoid being hit altogether.

Sophia was sent flying to the ground at Carson's feet, while the melon head ricocheted into the living room opening, snarling and shaking its head.

The thing squatted, poised for another attack, but did not move. Instead it spread its mouth wide and unleashed a vicious, foghorn-like croak that echoed in the room. Carson immediately recognized the behavior from the movie and braced himself for what should happen next...

The window behind the monster exploded into a hundred pieces as a second melon head entered the fray. The first one took a step back and Carson knew that meant the second was coming. And he'd be the target this time.

Remembering how it worked from the movie—which even in the split second of reaction time he had, he knew was insanity, trusting the logic of a movie—Carson willed himself to be brave. If he was right, all he had to do was get one good shot in at the monster. Prevent his own killshot. Stay alive.

The second melon head took the several quick strides it needed to reach Carson and dove at his legs. Carson jumped, narrowly clearing the outstretched claws and distended head.

He landed, spun, and slashed in one motion, hoping his aim was correct. It was close enough.

The tip of the blade sliced into the monster's laid out back, opening up a half-foot long gash. Rotten, black-green blood oozed out.

The monster screeched, a terrible and brutal wail, then scrambled up and away from Carson. Sophia was back on her feet, back to back with Carson again. Each faced a monster, one in the living room, one backing down the hall. Both monsters started chattering, squawking some unknown language, then fled, retreating the way the other had come.

Carson waited a few extra seconds after hearing the monsters leave, then turned, panting, to Sophia. She was bent at the waist, gripping her left arm with her right hand. Concerned, he started to ask if she was okay, then saw her grin and stopped.

She stood upright and laughed. "What a rush."

Carson blinked at her, wide-eyed. "You're insane."

Sophia gave him a face that said *meh, maybe*, then said out loud: "They were checking for weak spots, right? Just like the movie."

"It seemed that way. . . Wow. I can't believe this is happening."

"Well, I'm glad the fleeing part was real too. That

gives us a second to regroup. How long until they attack again do you think? Couple minutes?"

"Yeah, not much more I'd say."

"Are you ready?" she asked.

"Man, I don't know." Carson breathed heavily, feeling their time slip away. "Do you think we'll be able to keep defending ourselves this way?"

"We don't have a choice, do—"

Sophia stopped mid-sentence, and Carson saw in her eyes that she realized the same thing he just had.

"Do you have gas in here?" she asked.

Carson shook his head. "There's a lighter in the drawer under the knives, but the gas is in the shed outside, and I'm not going out there."

"Then how?"

"I've got it," Carson said. And he had. "Grab the lighter."

He sprinted down the hall to the third door on the right. The bathroom.

First drawer, second drawer, third drawer nothing. Medicine cabinet. . . bingo.

Carson snatched what he was looking for and ran back to Sophia. She held up the lighter in her hand, he held up the can of hairspray in his.

"Think it will work?" she asked.

"It's going to have to."

CHAPTER SIX

With no room for error now, Carson and Sophia retreated to the basement and shut themselves into the bathroom within. Fully aware that they were effectively backing themselves into a corner, they also knew it was the only place in the house where they could hope to trap the monsters. No access to the outside from the bathroom (or vice versa); only one way in, one way out. And Carson and Sophia would be waiting with the best weapon they had.

Fire.

The only foolproof method for killing melon heads in the movie.

Not long after they entered the bathroom, locked the door, and took their positions, the melon heads came back. Through the air vents, Carson and Sophia could hear more glass shattering—they were entering in different ways than the first time.

From there it sounded to them like the monsters were systematically searching the upstairs, forcing and breaking and pushing aside anything that stood in their way. The melon heads were leaving no stone unturned to find the prey they knew were hiding inside.

Several minutes passed as they destroyed the upstairs, but eventually the commotion descended, coming close. Almost time.

A sudden crash against the door ripped an involuntary yelp from Carson's lips. He squeezed the grill lighter and hairspray can in each hand, checking his finger position on each button trigger.

The melon head rammed the door again, cracking the cheap manufactured wood in two.

Silence. From Carson thanks to considerable effort. From Sophia due to her incredible resolve. From the melon head because of what it saw at that moment. . .

Sophia, waiting.

It attacked. Two strides and a dive at Sophia.

The melon head collided head first with Sophia's reflection in the bathroom mirror. Dazed, it mewled. Carson sprung forth out of the tub, igniting the lighter, holding it out in front of him toward the monster. He sprayed the can into the flame.

The monster lit up like a dead Christmas tree, the sudden greenish-orange blaze knocking Carson back.

It screamed. A thousand dying wails. Carson started to put his hands to his ears, block out that horrible noise, but before he could be heard, in succession: a *thwap*, a screech, and Sophia yelling his name.

Carson spun to find Sophia swinging at the second melon head, making contact, but fruitlessly. He knew what he had to do, but Sophia was too close to the monster. She'd get burned along with it.

Carson shouted at the monster, trying to get its attention. No luck. It was dead set on Sophia, clawing at her now. Sophia screamed. Blood spatter flew across the small room.

No time.

He jumped at the thing, wrapping his arm around it in a sort of headlock. He dug his heels in and yanked backward, away from Sophia.

The melon head chomped onto his forearm as they toppled over.

Carson yelled. A hundred miniature razor blades tearing at his flesh. The hairspray and lighter flew from his hands, skittering across the tile floor.

Panic. But the pain momentarily cleared his focus. He could feel the immense power rippling through the small monster's body. This was not a fight he could win on strength alone.

He rolled, wrestling with the melon head. One second with his back on the floor, the next second on top of the monster. All the while it clamped down on his arm.

Sophia roared, her aggression and adrenaline palpable, and took a lumberjack swing. Carson felt more than saw the bat *whoosh* past his face and connect with the monster.

It wasn't much, but it was enough.

Carson ripped his arm free of the melon head's clenched jaws—losing more flesh in the process—and was able to scramble away.

"Get the—" he started, but Sophia already had them. So instead he shouted, "Now! Do it now!"

She brandished the lighter, had the aerosol can at the ready.

Sophia clicked the ignitor.

And nothing happened.

The melon head hopped up onto its feet, swinging its head wildly between Sophia and Carson, debating which to attack.

Click, click, click. Sophia tried again and again. She looked to Carson, bewildered, pained. . . scared.

Time was being sluggish, but there was still not enough for Carson to speak. His eyes did the talking, though, protruding from his skull, imploring his cousin to try, try again.

She did.

Click. Hsst. Whoosh.

The melon head went up in flames, bright as the sun in the close quarters of the bathroom, and in seconds became a pile of ashes.

The threat was over.

Carson looked to Sophia. She, wide-eyed, looked back. They sighed so loud it echoed in the bathroom and then burst into hysterical laughter.

"We did it. Can you believe it?" Carson asked.

"No, I really can't. *Oww*, damn. That second one got me pretty good." She pointed at her cheek to a scratch and tilted her right shoulder forward where a gash had torn through her sleeve and into her skin.

"No kidding," Carson said, lifting his shredded forearm for Sophia to see. "It ought to be fun explaining this to the hospital."

They stepped over the remains of the door and made

their way upstairs. Carson whistled. "To think I planned to move into this place. A tornado might have done less damage."

The living room looked like ground zero. Not a single piece of furniture remained intact. Broken glass covered the floor. The TV smashed beyond recognition. Yet, miraculously, the front door was in place and whole, the lock still engaged. "Figures," Carson muttered, then stepped into the kitchen to see the score there.

"You're moving back?" Sophia asked.

But Carson didn't answer. He was too distracted by what he found in the kitchen. "Oh, come on!"

"What? What's wrong?"

"My laptop—they destroyed it." He pointed a hand to either side of the room, to the chunks of his busted computer that had been on the island counter and now strewn across the yellowed linoleum floor.

"You need that for your work, huh?"

"Unless you can think of another way to do web design."

"Can't you... I don't know, just buy a new one?"

Carson groaned. "I mean, yeah. I can. But I'm not exactly flush with a couple grand in cash."

"What, you don't think you can explain what happened to it to your boss?" She laughed, then must have seen the discontent plastered on his weary face because she quickly added, "Well, you will be getting an inheritance from Gran, right? And if it takes a while to get the money, I can loan you some, no problem. What do you say?"

Carson didn't say anything. A faint thud from somewhere at the back of the house caught his attention, although Sophia didn't seem to hear. *There is a third one.*

She started to speak again. Carson quickly put his hand up over her mouth. She recoiled with annoyance and a measure of disgust, then her eyes widened.

Carson pulled his hand back. His mind racing for a plan, eyes scanning the room. He saw his keys on the counter nearby and decided to grasp at straws. He whispered to Sophia, "Where are your keys?"

She pointed at her bag on the table.

He grabbed his own and nodded. "We're leaving."

Carson waited until Sophia could sidle over to the table and shoulder her bag. Another, louder crash came. Carson hit the button on his fob.

His car, tucked inside the garage on the opposite side of the ranch home, erupted into the blaring horns of its car alarm.

They ran. Carson hit the front door first, snapping the lock back and wrenching the door open. Sophia took off. She raced down the walkway to her SUV parked on the street, her bag slapping lightly on her back as she ran. Carson trailed closely behind, leaving the door wide for fear of drawing the hopefully preoccupied monster's attention with a slammed door.

Sophia had to skirt around the vehicle to get to the driver's side. She reached it about the same time Carson reached the passenger side. She scrambled inside, too busy with the key at the ignition to immediately realize Carson was still locked outside.

He smacked his hand flat against the window several times, catching her attention. Wide-eyed, she saw the problem and frantically searched for—and struggled to find—the unlock button on the door. Carson shot a glance over his shoulder toward the racket of his squealing car, desperate to see a sign of his distraction working. To his brief delight, he witnessed the third melon head ramming into the garage door with cracking metallic bangs. The aluminum bent and crumpled with relative ease from the force of the melon head but appeared to be holding long enough to keep its attention.

From the corner of his eye, Carson saw movement. He wheeled farther, coming back to face the house and its wide-open front door. An opening suddenly occupied by *another* melon head, feet scraping and teeth gnashing.

"Jesus, how many are there." He tried the door handle behind him, but it was still locked. "Come on Sophia. *Come on.*"

The melon head reared back and blatted that foghorn croak. The one at the garage stopped its assault, turning to notice Carson for the first time. A second passed, then they both charged.

Carson turned his back on them, knowing they'd cross the thirty or so feet of yard in no time. Sophia was reaching across the seat now, trying to push the door open as Carson took his last opportunity.

This time it opened. He pulled it back and leapt in, yanking the door closed behind him an instant before one of the melon heads slammed into it, rocking the SUV with the impact.

"Drive!" Carson yelled.

Sophia threw it in gear and stomped on the gas, the

tires spinning and squealing on the dewy blacktop before finding purchase and launching them off down the road. In the side mirror, Carson could see there were three monsters now, giving chase. But Sophia drove fast, not slowing down. Once the gap widened, their pursuers slowed, then peeled off out of sight into the night.

Only then did Carson slouch back and exhale heavily.

CHAPTER SEVEN

"Where are we going?" Carson asked.

"We should get first aid supplies for our wounds. No telling what diseases we might get from those monsters if we don't clean them out. But, after that, no clue. I figure the more miles between us and Gran's house the better."

Carson tiredly nodded his approval. "Damn that was close. What was up with the door lock? Trying to leave me out there for bait?"

"I'm sorry! I always have trouble finding the damn lock in this car."

Carson waved a hand. "I made it, at least. But you've got one hell of a dent in your car now." The melon head had hit the door hard enough to push some of the paneling tight up against the passenger seat.

"Oh God, is it bad?"

"Let's just say I hope you have good car insurance."

Sophia scoffed. "And tell them what? A fictional monster from a movie did it?"

"Well, I was thinking you could tell them it was a

deer, but sure, if you want to try the melon head route, go right ahead."

The two made quick eye contact then broke into fits of laughter. Eventually they lapsed into silence; Carson feeling okay despite his torn-up arm. He knew the adrenaline would completely fade soon, though, and the pain would be hell. He looked to Sophia and noticed her left arm resting limply in her lap. "Hey, is your arm okay?"

She lifted it weakly, winced, then let it fall into her lap again. "Hurts like a bitch, but I don't think anything is broken or torn. I can move it fine if I ignore the pain."

"We should get you some Ibuprofen or something then when we stop."

"Actually. . . I have something else that will work. Can you get the Altoids container from my bag? I have some pills in there."

"Sure," Carson said with a bit of side-eye. "Your standard, over-the-counter pain meds, no doubt."

"Something like that."

Carson pulled the backpack purse from the center console into his lap, unclipping the main flap to peer inside. His sole task was immediately interrupted when he saw the VHS tape.

"Hold on, you've had this in your bag the whole time?" he asked, removing it.

Sophia checked what he was holding. "Well, yeah. Where else would it be? I didn't take it out when I got home, and since it doesn't have legs it stayed there. And I bring my bag with me everywhere. Hence—" She gestured to the tape. "I mean, really. It doesn't take a genius to figure it out, Car. What is—"

"All right, hold on," Carson said, patting the air between them as if to apply brakes to the conversation. "I don't know what, exactly, but seeing this tape in your bag jogged something in my memory. A thought or a question, maybe?" He shook his head and groaned. "My brain feels rattled from everything that happened. I'm not thinking clearly. But whatever it is, I feel like it's important."

"It has something to do with me having the tape?"

"Yeah, I think so. A question about this whole mess, something specifically regarding you. But, what. . ."

"Like why those fuckers attacked me first, at my dad's house, instead of going after you in the house where we watched the movie?"

"Oh shit, yes. That's it! Have you been thinking that this whole time?"

"Well, the thought did cross my mind, but I couldn't figure out why. . ."

"Because they followed the tape!" they exclaimed simultaneously.

Carson slumped back in his seat again. "Damn. It does make some kind of sense, doesn't it?"

"Seems like it."

"Then I guess we know what to do," he said, pressing the window button. The glass lowered about a third of the way before coming to a halt, presumably hitting a bent track. But no problem, Carson had enough room to pass his hand and the VHS through, the wind of traveling eighty on the highway nearly yanking the tape from his hand before he had a chance to consciously let go.

"Wait!" Sophia shouted, tugging at Carson's close arm.

Carson pulled his hand inside, the tape still clutched in his fingers. "What?"

"What if the tape doesn't break when you throw it? We can't take any chances. We have to destroy it for good."

"All right, yeah. Let's make sure."

The next sign along the highway indicated they had already put several miles between them and the monsters. Carson wondered if Sophia had picked this direction of travel intentionally or not. He wondered if she realized she was taking them in the direction of the lakeshore and the supposed source of the monsters that attacked them. He was about to ask when she indicated her intention of exiting the highway. Carson saw the 24-hour grocery store a short way down the road and knew that was their destination.

They bought bandages and rubbing alcohol, thankful for the obscene hour so they wouldn't have to worry about drawing attention to themselves. They took turns dumping the alcohol on each other's wounds, hissing at the immediate and powerful sting, but feeling better for it. They wrapped Carson's forearm and bandaged the gash on Sophia's shoulder. The scratch on her cheek had stopped bleeding, so they left it. Carson said she might get a nice long scar out of it, but Sophia didn't seem to mind. If anything, she looked proud. A battle wound.

After, they took the tape from the car and moved to a spot better shielded from the store and the few patrons.

Carson set it on the parking lot asphalt. He held his hands up to Sophia and asked, "Care to do the honors?"

"Sure," she said, then stomped on the tape with the heel of her shoe. The first attempt made a satisfying *crack*, but she kept going, stomping so many times that Carson lost count. When she finally stopped, the black plastic of the tape body was in a hundred pieces, the ribbon a shredded and tangled mess.

"Should we burn it just in case?" Sophia asked.

"I didn't bring the lighter with me. Actually, I didn't grab any of that stuff on the way out."

"Me neither."

"I'm sure that's good, though," Carson said. "Nobody will be watching that thing again."

They both stared at the debris for a while, not speaking. The moonglow cast an eerie shimmer on the shiny ribbon.

Eventually, Sophia said, "So... that's it, right?"

"I think so?"

"Then why does it feel like it's not?"

"You too, huh?" Carson replied. He looked at the ruined fragments of the tape on the pavement once more and it reminded him of the case he found it in before. It gave him an idea.

"Should we call Isaac?" he asked.

"Your old burnout buddy? Why?"

"He's the only other person I know of who might have seen the tape before it ended up at Gran's house. So, I say we see if he knows anything about it."

As Carson retrieved his phone from his pocket,

Sophia asked, "Are you going to call him right now? It's barely after four in the morning."

"He works the overnight shift at the front desk of a hotel in the Holland area. If he isn't awake, he should be."

"I didn't know you two kept in touch."

"We don't. He just tweets nonstop when he's bored on the graveyard shift. So, like, all the time. The dude's a bit wacko, but his tweets are funny."

Carson scrolled through his contacts until Isaac came up. He dialed and turned it to speaker. Isaac answered on the third ring.

"Hello?"

From that single word, Carson could already tell the dude was stoned. "Hey Isaac, it's Carson. Carson Webber."

"No shit, Carson? It's been a helluva long minute since I've heard from you. What's good, my man?"

"Oh, you know. Things are, umm. . . Yeah, all right, I guess. Hey, I'm here with Sophia. You remember her, right?"

"Sophia, yeah! How could I forget a tasty piece of—"

"Hey, Isaac," Sophia said, interrupting him. "You're on speaker."

"Dude, come on," Carson added.

"What? There ain't nothing wrong with telling a woman she looks good."

"That is not—" Carson started, then saw Sophia holding a hand up.

"Isaac, we need your help. Something. . . is

happening and you might be the only one who can help us."

"Sure, yeah. This is the absolute least likely time for someone to check in, and I don't have to open up breakfast for almost two hours. Lay it on me."

Sophia nodded to Carson to go ahead with the story. Carson nodded back.

"Do you remember that box of VHS tapes you gave me? Basically the entire horror section from Movie Gallery?"

"Hell yeah I remember those. Man, I miss that job. And I miss renting movies from video stores. And hell, I even miss—"

"Yeah, me too," Carson said, knowing if he didn't cut him short he was likely to drag on. "Anyway, I just found one of the movies from that collection. *Critters*."

"Classic."

"Sure, never seen it. But that's not the point. The point is the movie inside the case was not *Critters*. It was one of those blank tapes that you could record to. It had a different movie on it, and the label said *Revenge of the*—"

"Melon Heads," Isaac finished. "Oh, fuck. I thought that was destroyed. You're not yanking my dick, are you?"

"No, we're not. There's more, though. It's going to sound crazy, but—"

"Did you watch it?"

"Yeah, we watched it. That's why we called—"

"Fuck, no. Don't tell me. I don't want to hear it," Isaac said, his voice suddenly quieter, but carrying a harshness that Carson didn't think Isaac was capable of showing.

"What does that mean?" Sophia asked.

When Isaac didn't respond right away, Carson said, "Look, man, we need your help. We're not far from you right now, so maybe we can stop by and talk about it."

"Whoa, hold on. Wait just a—"

Isaac's voice cut out. Carson and Sophia stood in silence for a few seconds before Carson said, "Isaac? You there?"

Nothing. Carson touched the screen, but it did not light up. He pressed the power button a couple times.

"Oh, shit. Battery died. Do you have a charger, by chance?"

"I don't," Sophia said. "Should we call him back with my phone?"

"We could if I had his number memorized. Which I don't."

"It was just displayed on your screen. You can't remember it from that?"

"Can *you*?" Carson challenged.

"Fair enough. Should we call the hotel then?"

"Nah, we're less than ten minutes away from there. And you heard him, he said he's got nothing going on for a while. Let's just go visit him."

CHAPTER EIGHT

"Are you really thinking about moving back into Gran's house?" Sophia asked, disrupting the quiet that had settled in around them in the few minutes after they were back on the road.

"Let's say I'm strongly considering it." Carson said, shifting in his seat to face her. Sophia's phone chimed in to tell her to turn left in five hundred feet. "That is, if the melon heads haven't torn it to the ground already *and* we somehow manage to survive long enough for me to move in."

Sophia laughed. "That's cool, Car. Hard to believe, though, after a decade on the move, you're finally coming home—well, sort of home."

"No, you're right. This is home. I spent most of my time here clinging to the fragments of my life before my mom died, and when that failed I swung the complete opposite way. I wanted so badly to leave this place behind. I'd convinced myself it was family that was the problem, constant reminders of my mom and the life that was stolen from me. Took me ten years of running and never settling to realize I had it dead wrong. Gran and Gramps. Your dad. *You*. I should never have left in the first place."

"Eh, I wouldn't beat yourself up about it, Car. You had to figure it out for yourself, and that takes time. You're here now."

"But I wasn't here when I should have been. I mean, Christ, I barely remember Gramps' funeral. I think I was only here a few hours total. I damn sure wasn't here for Gran like she deserved. I wasn't here for her at the end, either. . ."

"Hey, come on. Don't do that. I promise Gran loved you and never held it against you. She knew as well as anyone who you really are. There's a reason she left you the house."

"Because there was no one else left. Everyone else has an established life already." He laughed, but he could hear his exhaustion in it. "Maybe it was meant to be punishment, cleaning all that junk up."

"You know as well as I do that that's simply not true. And Gran knew that you care deeply, but you're a roamer. Until it's time to come home. And it sounds like that time is now. Ignore the circumstances for a minute. You're here now. You're home."

"Thanks, Sophia. I am home. Even after all that time trying so hard to stay away, I knew eventually I had to come back for Gran. If not in life, then to do what needed to be done after she's gone. I forgot there for a bit, but on some level, I've always known just how much Gran did for me, and how much she cared about me. It couldn't have been easy to step in as a mother figure to an eight-year-old."

"No shit. Gramps did help, though."

"Of course, yeah. Your dad did too. How's he doing, by the way? I chatted with him briefly at the funeral but he seemed a little closed off."

"He's doing okay. Gran passing has been hard, of course. And with me not super close by anymore. . . it was just him and Gran left around here, you know?"

"Yeah, I know," he said. "I didn't see your mom at the funeral. You guys still. . .?"

"That bitch is dead to me."

Carson nodded. "Fair enough. Just wondered."

"Look, if someone as ancient as Gran could find a way to accept me, then the woman who birthed me has no excuse."

"Completely agree," he responded, then quickly moved on. "Hey, if I do end up staying at Gran's, will that convince you and Rae to move back to this side of the state? Your dad and I would love it!"

Sophia smiled and gave a slight shrug. "You never know. I think I'd love it too."

The hotel loomed ahead. Sophia pulled into the parking lot, finding a space close to the entrance. Isaac stood outside the front door, smoking a cigarette in quick, jabbing motions. Carson recognized him immediately, though not because Isaac hadn't changed in the decade since he'd last seen the guy in person—but because now, with a little more weight, a little less hair, and a pair of glasses instead of the contacts he wore in high school, Isaac looked like a carbon copy of his dad. Not that Carson would ever say so to Isaac, because that would surely send the guy into an existential crisis.

Which, from a quick judgment of Isaac's appearance, he might already be there.

They parked and got out, headed toward Isaac. It took a second for him to realize who they were, then he took a huge drag on his cig, crushed it under his shoe, and immediately pulled a fresh one from the pack in his pocket.

"Whoa, Isaac, are you okay, man?" Carson said watching his old friend struggle to light the smoke with shaking hands.

"You shouldn't have come here," Isaac said.

"Gee, good to see you too."

Isaac pawed at some bristly stubble on his chin. "No, that's not what I meant. You two are dangerous to me now. Oh, God. What a fuckin' night."

"You're telling us," Sophia said. The scrunched brow and flat gaze told Carson she wasn't impressed by his plan thus far.

"Yeah, what's up with you, Isaac?"

"Me? What's up with *me*? The melon heads, that's what!" The last part came out loud, causing Isaac to shrink within himself briefly, check around to see if anyone heard him. There was no one. "I assume you didn't get rid of them? Huh? They're still out there?"

Carson looked to Sophia, then back to Isaac. "So you do know. I *knew* you'd know."

Isaac had since given up trying to light his cigarette. Instead he glared, bug-eyed, at Carson. "Are they still out there or what?" he hissed.

"Chill, man. We killed a couple, but yeah, they are.

They're way back at our grandmother's place, though. Like twenty miles from here."

Isaac shook his head, laughing humorlessly. "You two have no idea. You're clueless!"

"No shit!" Sophia shouted. "That's why we're here, so you can help us."

He glanced at Sophia, his eyes sad and pitiful. "Why me? I don't want to be a part of this. I didn't ask for that."

"Who else were we supposed to go to?" Carson asked. "I got this tape from you, man."

Isaac exhaled a heavy, stale breath. "Right. Well, come on inside then."

CHAPTER NINE

C arson and Sophia followed Isaac into the lobby, around the front desk, and through a door the color of smoke with an "Employees Only" sign. Along the way, Carson questioned whether Isaac should be absent from his post at the front desk, and all he got as a response was a finger pointed at the bell on the counter.

The office was small, made smaller by the clutter. At the plain, paper-strewn metal desk there was a rolling office chair that once was black but now worn through mostly white. The only other chair was of the folding variety positioned at the far end of the desk with a box of tourist pamphlets from local businesses. Isaac made no attempt to make room for them, instead collapsed into the office chair, leaving Carson and Sophia standing around awkwardly.

The computer monitor on the desk showed a program for viewing security cameras, but each box was black with the words "NO SIGNAL." Carson pointed at the screen. "Shouldn't those cameras be. . . showing something?"

"I told management weeks ago something was broken," Isaac said, shrugging. "Guess they don't care."

"Nice," Carson said, then they all went quiet for a minute.

"Well?" Sophia asked, breaking the silence.

"What do you want to know?" Isaac said wearily.

"Tell us everything you know," Carson replied. "Anything and everything relevant to this madness."

"Honestly, I don't know much."

"Then it shouldn't take long, should it?" Sophia said.

Carson shot her a look that was probably too simple to explain its complexity: *I know you're frustrated. I am too. Just. . . give the guy a second. We need him.*

"Okay, I don't know, how about start from the beginning?" Carson said. "When you first heard about the tape, et cetera."

Isaac nodded, his eyes cast down to the scuffed and dirty floor.

"We found the tape in the storage room of the video store. Matt Jackson did, actually."

"Matt Jackson worked at Movie Gallery with you?" Carson asked.

"Yeah, but not for long."

"Wait," Sophia said. "Matt Jackson? Isn't he the kid that ran away from home? Did the police ever find him?"

Isaac looked up finally. "Matt didn't run away."

"What do you mean? I remember seeing it on the news. Everyone knew Matt ran—"

"Holy shit," Carson said. "Did he. . . ?"

Isaac nodded.

"How do you know for sure? Wait, have you watched the movie?"

"I never watched it. Do you think I'd still be here if I had? But I know what happened to Matt because I saw it happen. I watched those fucking monsters rip the kid to pieces."

"Holy shit," Carson said again. "How? How did you...?"

"Survive? I don't know, not exactly. Matt and I were supposed to work the closing shift one night, but he never showed. It was storming pretty bad, so who knows, we thought maybe he had something going on at the house he had to fix. In any case, the boss eventually got Ben Chambers to fill in. Ben and I worked the shift, completely uneventful, until we got a call just before closing time. It was Matt. He sounded panicked, terrified. Said he'd watched the dumb melon head movie and now they were after him. I thought he was just messing with us. I mean, for God's sake, he told us, 'They know I've seen the tape.'"

Isaac suddenly slammed his hand down hard on his thigh, the flat report resounding off the close walls. Sophia jumped at the noise. After a few moments, Isaac continued.

"The call got disconnected, but Ben and I, we didn't think anything of it. Just finished out our shift and closed shop. We'd just turned out the lights and were locking the front door when Matt showed up on foot in the pouring rain. He didn't live far from the store, if you remember where his folks' place was, but he looked like he'd been running for his life." Isaac swallowed hard with an audible click, before finishing. "He was maybe ten feet from the door, calling for us, when they got him."

"Oh my God," Sophia whispered.

"God had nothing to do with it," Isaac said, his head shaking with disgust.

"So," Carson said carefully, feeling the tension lingering in the cramped office. "What happened then? How did the tape end up back at Movie Gallery?"

"We didn't think it was real, not at first. How could we? That shit doesn't happen in real life. I think the rain washing all the gore off the pavement into the sewer drain helped us in thinking it wasn't real, you know? Like, how do you ignore a giant pool of blood and bits of Matt ten feet from the front door if they're just piled up there? But the rain did a hell of a job cleaning up the mess. That, and the melon heads themselves didn't leave much of anything behind. We were shell-shocked. So much so that we told ourselves we couldn't believe our own eyes. Crazy, right? I didn't sleep that night, but I think by morning I'd come to believe it never happened.

"Then a day later the cops showed up at the store. Ben and I were working a shift together again, and the cop asked if we'd heard from Matt. His parents were worried because he'd gone missing. I don't know if we were still in denial or what, but we both clammed up. Somehow, we both managed to say the same thing at the same time, that we thought he'd run away. Surprised the hell out of me and Ben but it seemed to confirm a suspicion the cops had. You know those local bumpkins. They'd do anything to get out of doing actual police work. Well, anyway, that was that. One short question-

and-answer with us and the story was out. Matt had run away, and no one ever saw him again. Except by now, Ben and I knew what we saw was real, and that the only reason we were still alive was because we happened to turn the lights out just before Matt and the monsters arrived. The melon heads never saw us."

Isaac fumbled a cigarette from his pocket, started to light it, then finally realized where he was and left it hanging limp from his lips, looking sad like a hit mutt. At last he plucked it from his mouth and stuffed it back into the pack.

"Well, no one ever knew what really happened besides us. As far as I know Ben never told anyone, at least not while he was still living around here. He moved his ass out to Cali—probably because of the damn things. He was scared shitless, and so was I. *Fuck*, I'm starting to regret not doing the same thing. . ." Isaac grunted, shook his head. "Anyway, you're the first people I've ever spoken to about this."

He didn't say anything for a minute after that, seeming to think something over.

"As far as the tape getting back to the store, I honestly didn't know it had. Not until you called. I assumed it got destroyed or lost or whatever along with Matt, but now I think I know what happened. Not long after Matt disappeared—died, whatever—his dad stopped by the store with a small box of movies. From what I remember, Matt's folks coped in drastically different ways. Matt's mom wanted to believe he was still out there. Probably still does to this day. But his dad, man, he wanted all of Matt's shit gone. He couldn't handle the sight of any of it. You know it was because it tore him up inside emotionally, but he was the classic type of man from around here. Hardened, no bullshit type. He wanted Matt's stuff gone because he knew it threatened his outward appearance of being strong and unemotional. Well, whatever, but I saw through his facade that day he stopped by with the box. The guy was a wreck, barely holding himself together. We didn't really accept donations at the time, especially not VHS tapes since we were basically all DVD by then, but what was I supposed to say? I took the box, figuring I'd leave it out in the break room fair game for anyone to pick through.

"Never stuck out to me at the time, but now I remember there was a handful of rental copies in the box of Matt's stuff. I figured they were copies he rented with his discount or straight up stole, but again, we had all but phased out the VHS tapes by then, so I just tossed them into the pile of old tapes in the storage room. Most of that shit vanished over time, but the melon head video —disguised in what, the *Critters* case?—must have ended up in the collection I started for you, Carson."

"Then it just so happened to get lost from the box in Gran's closet after she confiscated them from me, sitting there ever since," Carson said. "Wow."

Sophia had leaned back against a small patch of bare wall during Isaac's story, but came forward now. "It's a hell of a story, I'll give you that, but nothing you've told us so far actually helps us out in our current situation."

"Sophia!"

"What?" she said, turning on Carson. "Am I wrong?

In case you somehow managed to forget, those goddamn monsters attacked us less than an hour ago. We could be dead already if we hadn't fought our way out."

Carson didn't know how to respond. He knew she was right. His thumbnail found his lip again as he chewed on the situation, wondering again just how in the hell they were supposed to get clear of this mess.

Isaac breathed noisily. "Okay, I have a theory. But, bear in mind, the entire thing is complete speculation based on what I witnessed and what little I could find on the internet."

"Yeah, sure. It's better than what we have right now," Carson said.

"Do you still have the tape?"

"No, we smashed it," Sophia said.

Isaac bobbed his head up and down a couple times. "I would have too. But it won't make a difference."

"What do you mean?" Carson asked.

"You might have saved someone else's life by destroying the tape, but that won't help you. I think they're able to track you initially because of the tape, but once they find you. . . Well, you're both marked now. They'll keep coming for you."

"How do you know?"

"Something I read on the internet."

"And you believe it?" Sophia asked.

Isaac shrugged, as though whether he believed it or not was inconsequential.

"Fine. I'm not sure I buy it, but let's say you're right. Why, then?" Sophia asked. "Why are they after us? Just for watching a movie?"

"I think because that movie exposes their existence."

"Wait, I thought the movie was supposed to have created or summoned them or whatever. That's what the guy at the end said. The guy who made the film." Carson said.

"I'm sure it did. They made a movie about an urban legend and made it real. And now that the melon heads are real, they want to survive. You two seeing the movie threatens that. Threatens *them*. You're a liability now."

"I don't know, this all seems so crazy," Carson said, rapping his knuckles against the metal desk with a hollow clang. "It doesn't make any sense to me."

"Does it have to?" Isaac asked.

"Yes!" Carson yelled suddenly. "This isn't some B movie from the '80s, man. This is *real life*."

"Look, don't blame me. I didn't make the rules, if there even are any. Besides, we're talking monsters that shouldn't exist. The logistics behind how or why they operate are a bit irrelevant, don't you think?"

"No, I don't think. Because we're trying to survive here. You know, figure out a way to stop them and walk away still breathing?"

Isaac, his head still hanging, looked at them over his glasses. "We won't survive."

"Jesus, what the hell," Sophia said, groaning into her hands.

"Look, I have no idea if there's a way to stop them. Did you say you killed some?"

"Yeah, with fire," Sophia said. "That's what worked in the movie, and it did for us too."

Isaac made a soft noise of approval, then said, "But more came after you?"

Sophia sighed. "Yeah."

"So how many are there then? Will they keep coming after you?" He shrugged, then went silent.

"I don't believe this," Carson said, turning to face the door. "Do you have *any* thoughts on what we can do now? Anything we could try to stop them."

Sophia spoke before Isaac could answer. "We have to kill them all. Right, Isaac? It really is that simple, isn't it? We kill them all before they kill us?"

"Yeah, probably."

"Okay, but where?" Carson asked.

"Where else? The woods around Felt Mansion. Maybe you can surprise them."

"How in the hell are we supposed to surprise them if they already know where we are?"

"Well, from what I've read, they're nocturnal. You might be okay during the day."

"Might be?"

Isaac shrugged again, that maddeningly useless gesture.

Several seconds passed, then Sophia spoke. "You said 'we.' Why are you so scared of them if you didn't watch the movie?"

Isaac pushed his glasses back up his nose by its bridge. "Because you've dragged me into this by coming here. If they see me with you I'm dead, tape or not."

"Even if they are, which I'm not even sure we know that for sure, we left them miles behind. It would take them a long time to get here on foot, and I'm doubting they know how to drive a car."

Carson, still staring at the door, suddenly cocked his ear. Something beyond the door had caught his attention, but it was faint. "Hey, guys?"

Isaac either ignored Carson or didn't hear him, because he continued his back and forth with Sophia. "How long after watching the movie did they attack you? Huh?"

"I don't know, but—"

Listening intently now, with his eyes closed, Carson heard another noise. Not loud, but it sounded like something crashing or smashing.

"And how far away did they come from? Hmm? Farther than where you came from to here, I'll tell you that."

"Guys, do you hear that?"

Sophia persisted. "Look, I don't know the exact time or miles, but—"

"Guys!"

A sudden bang and subsequent explosion of tinkling, shattering glass provided an extra exclamation point.

Isaac chuckled resolutely. "They're here."

He sprang to the door.

CHAPTER TEN

"Isaac, wait! Don't!"

But Carson was too late. Isaac had the door open and was halfway out before Carson could finish saying the word *don't*. Carson leapt at the door, but whether he intended to grab Isaac and pull him back or slam the door shut to lock Isaac out, he wasn't sure. In either case, Isaac was out the door by the time Carson got there. The door opened out from the small office, and Carson let it swing most of the way closed, allowing for just enough space for him to peer out after his old friend.

Isaac made it clear of the desk and a step into the hall beyond at a half-crouch. He peered right, then left, then back right. Then he stood, sparing a glance over his shoulder at Carson, a confused expression scribbled on his disheveled face. Isaac shrugged—

A blur with a bulbous head flashed into view from Isaac's left, hitting the poor guy at alarming speed. Carson heard the monster's snarl an instant before Isaac's surprised *ooph* on impact.

Carson couldn't prevent the soft, mewling groan from escaping his own lips, but somehow managed to act before his brain staged a revolt at what he'd just seen. He leaned back, quickly and gently pulling the door shut. The latch snapping home sounded like a shotgun blast to Carson in his heightened sense of animal instinct, but he knew it was closer to nonexistent compared to the scene on the other side of the door. He eased the lock into place with another click.

"What? What happened?" Sophia said.

Spinning fast, Carson faced Sophia with a finger to his lips. As she nodded her acknowledgement, her eyes shining orbs in the harsh glare of the overhead fluorescents, Isaac shrieked, *"It's not fair! I didn't even watch the fucking tape!"* then unleashed a tortured scream. Carson squeezed his own eyes shut, his hands working their way to his ears to block out the haunted sound.

Isaac screamed for several more seconds before— mercifully, Carson initially thought—it came to an end. What he hadn't expected was the set of new sounds that followed in the scream's wake. Growling, gnashing and clacking teeth, wet and fresh ripping, snapping. Carson opened his eyes to see Sophia holding her mouth, her body in minor convulsions as she did what Carson suddenly had to do: fight back vomit in his throat.

Several seconds later the noises stopped. Carson finally was able to regain some composure, and it seemed Sophia had won her internal fight as well. The silence, though, only brought a different emotion to the surface. Fear.

"What do we do now?" Sophia whispered.

Carson moved to her, directing them both to the far side of the small space, facing the door. He leaned close to her ear and whispered back. "We can't risk going out that door, and there's nowhere else to go. I think we have to wait it out. I locked the door. Hopefully it holds."

"What about the desk? Should we move it in front of the door?"

Carson shook his head. "Not yet. I don't want to make any noise that will draw their attention."

They remained where they were for a few minutes, their bodies in varying degrees of protective and defensive postures, scrunched up against the wall, eyes locked on the door, ears strained to pick up any sign that the monsters still lurked in wait. The only noise Carson could hear for a long time was the thump of his rapidly beating, yet slowing, heart. He made to ask Sophia if he thought they had gone when one of the monsters smashed into the door.

The loud noise startled them both. Sophia cried out, while Carson jumped, snapping his head back into the concrete wall. A balloon of pain immediately flared up in his head, eyes watering and vision blurry. He tried shaking his head clear, but that only served to enhance the pain.

The melon heads attacked the door twice more in back-to-back crashes. The door shook heavily in its frame but, for the time being, held. Another quick attack left a dent visible from the inside in the center of the door.

"The desk! Quick!" Carson yelled. No reason to stay quiet now—the melon heads seemed intent on smashing their way inside regardless.

Without bothering to clear the desk, Carson and

Sophia each grabbed what they could of the metal desk, dragged it into the middle of the room, then flipped it on end. It was clumsy work, with the desktop computer and a smattering of papers and folders sent careening to the floor, but they pushed the desk up against the door, letting it tip angled between the two side walls on either side. For good measure, they shoved the two chairs up against it, knowing that would do nothing, but they had to try. All the while, the monsters attacked the door.

They backed away to the far wall again. Sophia chanted, "Oh my god oh my god oh my god."

"I know. We have to do something. I don't think the door will hold much longer."

"What, though?" she asked.

"Oh! Call the police!"

"And get them killed too?"

"You care? At least they have guns!"

She considered it for a second, then yanked her phone from her back pocket. She dialed 9-1-1 and waited, her foot ripping a drum riff on the tiled floor. Carson heard the line connect and the dispatcher on the other end say, "9-1-1, what's your emergency?"

Sophia clammed up, her mouth ajar, but no words came out. Instead she stared at the door, and immediately Carson knew what had caused her to freeze. They weren't believed the last time they called 9-1-1 about the melon heads, so what would make this time any different?

Carson snatched the phone from her hand as the dispatcher said, "Hello? Is anyone there? What's your emergency?"

"Hi, yes, sorry. I think someone is hurt. I heard loud. . . loud screaming. And a lot of other noise. Things smashing and breaking."

"Sir, where are you?

"We're at the Holiday Inn, north of—"

Another barrage of assaults against the door cut him off. And beyond that, someone screamed. *Isaac?*

"What was that? Sir, are you all right? Are you safe?"

"Ye—yes. I'm hiding out. But something terrible is going on. Send the police now!"

"Okay, sir. Please stay put if you are safe. We are sending officers to your location now. If you'll please stay—"

Carson hung up. "Good enough."

The attacks continued: so loud in the small office. Carson's head felt tapped and about ready to be split open. He thought he heard more screaming, but could no longer be sure they weren't phantom echoes of Isaac's screaming from several minutes earlier.

"How long will the door hold, do you think?"

"Hopefully long enough for the police to get here first," he replied.

As if Carson had purposely set out to jinx them, the next impact broke something loose. The door sunk in towards them, caught up on the upturned desk, but a fresh gap at the top corner of the door exposing the other side could be clearly seen. Carson gawked at the opening, his brain needing another jump to start again.

A gnarled and rubbery, sickly white-green face with dully glowing eyes the color of rust filled the space for a moment, before disappearing again.

"Holy shit. Sophia!"

Carson ran to the desk, throwing his body into the heap of metal. Something pointy jabbed the soft part of his side, causing him to cry out in pain, but he held the pressure. He might have been tempted to ease up if not for the sudden opposing force pushing back.

"Soph—"

She hit the desk next to him, both hands planted and pushing with considerable exertion based on the expression on her face. Carson renewed his efforts, putting everything he had into holding the desk firm. The monsters were strong, though. With every impact, Carson and Sophia were pushed back a few inches, requiring them to shove the desk forward again, forcing the door back mostly into its frame.

"I don't know how long I can hold on," Sophia said through clenched teeth.

"Me either," Carson grunted back.

Between the steady cacophony and the strain of pushing, his head swelled with pain. He squeezed his eyes shut against it, concentrating on the task at hand and nothing else. Soon everything went black. Not just his vision buried behind his eyelids, but everything else. The sounds faded as his adrenaline-fueled blood pulsed in his ears. The pain too, became a normal feeling that sunk into the background. As he pushed, blocking out the world around him, Carson wondered if the monsters got in, how long it would take to reach this empty plane of existence again. The ungodly pain of limbs being severed from his body would come first, of course, but he wanted to believe they would make quick work. The gentle void of death would arrive soon—

"Carson."

He blinked, opening his eyes. A dark, blurry glare remained for several seconds as his mind resurfaced along with his vision.

"Carson," Sophia said again, more urgently this time. She grabbed his shoulder, shaking him lightly.

His vision finally cleared, allowing him to see the concern twisting her face.

"Are you okay?" she asked.

"Yeah, I'm fine. What happened? What's going on?"

"Listen."

And he did. The assault on their makeshift bunker had ceased. Everything had gone eerily quiet in the wake of the raucous noise caused by the monsters. Except—

Sirens. Wailing nearby, growing stronger. Closer.

Only then did Carson realize Sophia was no longer pushing against the desk. He eased off, unsticking his side with the metal edge that had found a home there, the sudden relief nearly orgasmic. Carson took a step back, shaking out his arms and shoulders, feeling the stiffness creeping in, knowing his body would feel wrecked by morning.

Morning.

"Soph, what time is it?"

"Just after six, why?"

"Oh my God. Dawn."

"You think Isaac was right? That we're safe when it's light out?"

Carson shrugged. "Maybe?"

"What about the police sirens? You don't think they fled because of them?"

He shook his head. "I don't know, not for sure. But they left, right? And if you think about it, they're trying to kill us to keep their existence a secret. Wouldn't it make sense that they'd avoid the light?"

"I guess."

Carson shrugged again, then pulled the folding chair up to the desk. He stood on the seat and, hesitantly, peaked through the gap. There was no movement beyond, as expected.

"Here, help me with this."

He kicked the chair aside and, with the help of Sophia, took the desk away from the door. The door itself hung crooked in the frame and squealed when Carson tried to carefully push it open. He winced, waiting for the inevitable surprise attack from the monsters, but after nothing came several seconds later, he sidled his way out of the office with Sophia in tow.

Carson stopped halfway down the front desk, taking in the carnage around them. Tables and chairs overturned, couches shredded and tossed aside, and to top it off, the automatic sliding entrance doors obliterated into a sea of shimmering shards of glass. Isaac was nowhere in sight.

"Damn," she said. "Wait, there's someone there."

Carson, thinking it was Isaac, followed her gaze to legs—pants ripped and bloodied; not Isaac's—poking out from under a section of flipped over couch. "Oh my God."

He tried to hustle to them, but Sophia held him back with a hand on his shoulder before he got started.

"Leave it. I. . . I don't think they're attached anymore."

"Oh."

The emergence of voices caught their attention. Down the main hallway from the lobby various people slowly crept in, the first gawkers at the crime scene. Through the front doors, Carson could see two parked police cars, their sirens off now, but the lights strobed on, bathing the scene in red and blue.

"We have to get out of here," Carson said quietly. He moved past the desk into the side hallway, looking right, away from the lobby and the growing crowd. At the end of the hall was the indoor pool, the door propped open with a mop bucket. Above the door was an Emergency Exit sign. "This way."

He slipped on his next step, which forced him to grab the wall for balance. A blood slick was the culprit, smeared a few feet across the floor tiles and now adorned with a skewed footprint. Carson swallowed back the sudden mouthful of spit, and said, "Hey, uhh. . . let's keep an eye out for the melon heads, yeah?"

"Good call."

Carson led the way. He was aware that the quiet, slinking sort of manner he'd adopted made him feel like they were doing something wrong—and hell, maybe they were—but the last thing he wanted to do was get tied up answering questions from the police. In his personal experience, though limited, the men in blue always seemed to dislike the answers provided, as if they were only looking for *their* truth, not the *real* truth. And that happened with everyday normal shit. Start talking about urban legend monsters, and you might as well be asking to take cuffs on the wrist and a ride in squad car to the loony bin.

As he slipped through the propped open door, Carson's nostrils were instantly stung by the heavy, rank odor of chlorine. It's a universal smell, but one that carried extra weight for Carson, reminding him of all the years on the move with his mom before she passed. They always stayed at shitty motels or hotels, but most still had a pool. Filthy, disease-ridden cesspools in retrospect, but one of the few true points of happiness from that time, aside from his mother.

Carson hadn't realized he'd slowed, but Sophia pulled at his arm as she passed, heading for the far corner of the room to the emergency exit. When they reached the door, Sophia suddenly stopped.

"What?" Carson asked, then saw the placard affixed to the glass.

Emergency Exit Only – Alarm Will Sound

"I guess it won't make much difference now, will it?" Sophia said.

"Nope. Cops are already here. Let's get the hell out of this place."

The exit spit them out on the far side of the building. They walked the long way around and got to Sophia's vehicle from the opposite direction of the police cars. Not that it mattered much, because they seemed to be preoccupied with the mess inside.

"So, where to now?" Carson asked as they hopped into the SUV.

Sophia drove them out of the hotel parking lot, heading back the way they'd come, towards the highway. "Felt Mansion?"

Carson sighed. "Can we get some food first?"

"Oh, thank God you said that. I'm starving too. And I know just the place."

CHAPTER ELEVEN

"Urban legends are weird," Sophia said, setting her phone down to stir a packet of sugar into her coffee. "Most of the theories behind their origin don't even make sense."

"Like how a movie brought them to life makes sense?" Carson shifted to stretch his legs across his booth seat. He took a cautious sip of his own steaming coffee and was pleased to find it the perfect temperature, the kind of hot that is on the cusp of painful but holds wonderful heat. Sophia hadn't lied. This was a damn fine cup of coffee.

"All right, you got me there. I guess it doesn't matter now where they came from. We know we have to kill them all or we'll end up dead. *And*, we know how to kill them."

"Sounds overwhelming," Carson sighed.

"Hey, if those dipshits Jenny and Randy can do it, then so can we."

"You mean the *fictional* characters Jenny and Randy? And Randy *died*."

"He didn't have to." Sophia was grinning, that

devious look gracing the normally soft features of her face. She may have lost some of her mojo at the hotel with Isaac, but Carson could tell a part of her held excitement. She looked bound and determined to get some joy out of this, even if she had to steal it from the charred remains of melon heads. Yet, the oddest part was that she didn't seem aware she was even doing it.

"What's up with you?" Carson asked.

The grin faltered, faded. "What the hell are you talking about? What do you think is up with me? We're being chased by monsters that shouldn't exist."

He waved a hand at her. "No, that's not what I meant. That little smile just a moment ago. It was the same as back at the house, after we fended them off the first time. Like you were having fun."

"Oh, I was?" She looked down into her mug, shrugged. "Well, you know."

"No, I don't—"

The waitress returned with their food. An omelet for Sophia and a couple eggs over easy, shredded hash browns, and a side of bacon for Carson. They nodded their thanks and waited approximately one half second before tearing into the food.

Carson broke the eggs over the potatoes and scarfed a few bites. Around a fresh fork-full, he said, "Come on. What's going on? I want to know."

Sophia swallowed. "What if I don't want to say?"

Carson held both hands up, the one with the fork flinging a bit of egg. "All right. That's fine. I'm not trying to force anything out of you that you're not comfortable sharing."

"No, you're right. I'm just so used to deflecting all the time. But, you and I, we used to tell each other everything, didn't we?"

"I know I did."

"Yeah, I guess I kind of forgot what that was like."

Carson waited a beat, then said, "It has to do with Rae and whatever you didn't tell me earlier, right?"

"No! No, everything's fine with Rae." She cleared her throat. "Okay. . . I don't know. We're just both so busy all the time. She's been working on a huge project for GM these past several months, and I've been putting in a bunch of hours volunteering at the community garden on top of the day job."

"How is work, by the way? You're still at the City there, right?"

"It's a job. I like numbers, but it's a city finance department. Aside from budget time, not terribly stressful."

"That explains all the volunteer hours."

"Well, you know me."

Carson did. He knew exactly what she meant. Sophia was an outside gal. When they were younger she always wanted to be doing something outside, whether it was helping Gran with the small vegetable garden or spending weekends up north hiking and camping out. The only exception was to watch movies with him. Which is why when she took the job at the City a few years back Carson questioned the decision, but she had an explanation—or excuse: *It's Michigan. If you want a full-time job year-round, you'll end up in an office.*

"So, what then? You're feeling pent up? Antsy?"

She was mid-bite, then stopped. "Exactly! I'm not used to this all day, every day monotony, you know? I see all these places you've been traveling to and it makes me itch to do *something* outside the normal. I miss getting out there. I miss feeling alive."

"I promise you traveling all the time is not all it's cracked up to be. You know how hard it is to keep a consistent job moving around like that? I'm lucky I found remote work last year. Thank God for laptops." He groaned, remembering his was now in pieces. "Expensive sons of bitches, but convenient."

"Okay, maybe, but is it worse than staying put all the time?"

"Beats the hell out of me. I suppose a balance somewhere in the middle would probably be nice."

"Look, I know you think I'm a little crazy, but I don't have a death wish. I love Rae. I'm happy with her, really. And I absolutely want to get back to her. But, it feels nice to get the blood pumping again."

Carson took the last few bites of food, then washed it down with a gulp of coffee. "You're right. You are crazy."

For a second Sophia looked hurt, then Carson smiled and they both laughed. She chucked her napkin at him and that only made Carson laugh harder. It was genuine and refreshing, but also made him realize just how tired he was. Carson was about to mention it when she spoke.

"How many do you think there are?"

"No idea. A bunch, probably." Carson rubbed the side of his stubbly face. "I'll tell you what I do know, though. I need a shower, a change of clothes, and sleep."

"What, you want to go home?"

He groaned. "No, I'm not ready to deal with the carnage back there. Honestly, I'm surprised I haven't heard from anyone about that yet. The car alarm alone probably got the cops called."

"Your phone is dead, remember?"

"Oh shit, yeah. Crazy, I can't remember the last time I was awake and not glued to my phone. Kind of pathetic, huh?"

Sophia wasn't listening. She was staring at her own phone.

"What's up?"

She held the screen out so Carson could see. Her dad was calling.

"Are you going to answer?"

"I don't think I should. Do you? I know my dad is probably worried, but we've seen what happens when we pull people into this mess. . ."

Her phone stopped ringing. Instead of waiting to see if her dad left a voicemail, she powered the phone off. "We have to finish this now. You and me. We can figure out our story once—if—we get out alive."

It was out there now. A minor slip of the tongue, but Carson now knew it was on her mind. *If* they survive. Carson had done his best to ignore thinking that way. The absurdity of the situation helped, as did reminiscing and joking with Sophia, but it was hard to completely avoid the reality of the situation. Isaac was dead. Killed by these monsters. Survival was not a guarantee.

"You okay, Car?"

He hadn't realized how long he'd been quiet, eyes drifting out the window. "Yeah, sorry. Just thinking."

"About?"

He smiled, gave his best exaggerated sheepish expression. "About how I left my wallet at home."

"Well then I guess you have two choices. Either dine and dash or suck it up and work some hours in the back, cleaning dishes to make up for it."

"Sophia!"

"I'm kidding. I'll cover you this time. But you owe me, Webber. Big time."

After breakfast they found the nearest hardware store to re-up on supplies since they'd left everything at the house. When they got there, Sophia told Carson to stay put; she'd run in, grab the essentials, then be back out in no time.

"Essentials? Don't we just need a couple lighters and a spray can?" Carson asked.

"You've seen Evil Dead 2, right?"

"Of course. How is that relevant? Unless you're going to get your forearm chopped off and attach a flamethrower in its place, I'm not catching your drift."

"Okay, not that literal. But closer. You know how Ash does that? Goes into the shed and just finds exactly what he needs and puts it all together?" She pointed at her chest. "I'm like that. Swear to God."

"You're literally going into a store that has everything we could possibly need. I don't know, the analogy doesn't track."

"Ugh, God," she groaned. "You're impossible. All I'm saying is I know what we need—more than just a couple lighters—and I'm going to head in there and get it. Then we're going to slaughter these evil big-headed bastards."

"You know Ash summoned the evil on himself in that movie, right?"

"So did we," she said, shutting the door on him and flitting away into the store.

Carson got bored after about a minute of waiting and reached for his phone. After stupidly tapping the power button three times, he remembered—for the tenth time —that it was dead. Admittedly, and ashamedly, he was getting a little antsy not being able to use it, and he wondered if smartphone addiction was a real thing, and if so, was it possible to have withdrawal? He stared at the blank screen for a solid thirty seconds as he recalled Sophia's reasoning for turning off her own. She was right, of course. Involving others, being available to others, and so on—none of it would help. He tossed the phone in the glove box.

Five minutes passed since Sophia left and Carson felt a slight twinge of worry. Five minutes was hardly anything, but she made a point of saying she'd be in and out. He scanned the parking lot, but there was nothing to be seen. It was nearly empty, and not a single person or creature moved within sight. Which was to be expected, considering it was a Sunday in West Michigan. All the non-heathens were off attending church.

Another couple minutes later and Carson laid his head back. He reclined the seat as far as it would go, the rising sun shone through his windows, bathing him in a pleasant warmth. He was asleep seconds later, and out just long enough for the first scenes of a dream to invade his sleeping mind. Glowing eyes, rows of teeth, bloody footprints... screaming—

His screaming. He was awake. A noise startled him awake, his limbs flailing briefly, attacking nothing.

"Whoa, Carson! Are you all right?"

"Huh?" He twisted in the reclined chair, peering behind him to see Sophia through the open trunk. Just Sophia. No monsters. He relaxed, rubbing his eyes. "Yeah, sorry. Fell asleep. You scared me."

She hefted a couple bags into the back and tossed in a long broom handle. She closed the trunk and came around, while Carson righted his seat.

"Got everything then?"

"Oh yeah, you bet I did."

Carson stared, waiting. "Care to share?"

"You'll see when we get there."

"There?"

"We're going to Felt Mansion. You know that."

"We really have to, huh?"

"Buck up, bud. We're doing this."

CHAPTER TWELVE

The drive wasn't long. In less than ten minutes they exited the highway and soon turned down a road with a couple signs. One for Saugatuck Dunes State Park, the other for The Felt Estate.

"The Felt Estate," Carson whispered. "Right here, all this time. You've never been here before, right?"

"Nope. Doesn't seem like the kind of place you would go unless you lived nearby or were invited to a wedding at the mansion. You?"

"I haven't either. Can you give me the quick facts from your research earlier?"

"Sure. The mansion is supposedly haunted, first of all."

"Really? On top of melon heads, the place is haunted too?"

"Yep. The original owner and his wife. He—Dorr Felt —built the mansion in the '20s for his wife, but she died a few weeks later or something. Then he died the next year."

"Jesus."

"Yeah, so if ghosts are a real thing—can't rule that shit out anymore these days—this old building seems prime for a haunting."

Sophia slowed the vehicle as they came to a fork in the road. The Felt Estate to the left, the state park to the right. Sophia directed them left.

"That's not the mansion, is it?" Carson asked, pointing at a big red brick building set back off the road on his side.

"No, I believe that's the carriage house. *That's* Felt Mansion."

She gestured with her head as they rounded a curve, the road coming to an end just ahead. To the left was a vast dirt parking lot and, perched upon a hill to the right, was the mansion. The three-story building, bricked with an array of light browns and tans, boasted more windows than Carson could count, and multiple, thick chimneys jutted into the sky.

"Oh yeah," Carson said. "Looks pretty much the same as from the movie. Renovated a bit, maybe, but that's definitely it."

Sophia pulled the car into the dirt lot, parking towards the end by a quaint, white chapel. Beyond, the grounds opened wide, an expanse no doubt encapsulated in the view from the mansion. Carson had said he'd never been here before, but he was finding that in a weird way it wasn't exactly true. The more he observed his surroundings, the more he recognized from the movie. But even that recognition felt off, as if he were experiencing vivid déjà vu. Aspects seemed familiar but were skewed through the lens of a camera and over the course of three decades worth of time.

Carson noticed Sophia glancing out the rear window to the south, to a dark wall of forest.

"What's that way?" he asked.

"State park. It surrounds the whole estate. There's a network of trails throughout the trees that lead out to the dunes and Lake Michigan."

"And that's where. . ."

"Where the melon heads live, supposedly. Somewhere in the hundreds of acres of woods."

"I think I'd rather find Winnie the Pooh."

"That's a terrible joke," Sophia said flatly, exiting the car. Carson followed suit.

The wind was stiff this close to the lakeshore, but the minor bite felt nice to Carson, finally snapping him out of his tired funk. The parking lot had few cars in it, but in the first minute of standing outside the car, three more vehicles entered. The disc golf course that started just at the end of the parking lot, along with the trails to the lake, seemed to be a popular destination, no doubt fueled by a desire to get some recreation in before the bear of summer heat arrived around midday.

Sophia was at the back of the SUV, digging into the trunk. Carson came around and finally saw the supplies she bought at the hardware store. To go with the broom handle, there was: a stack of rags, kerosene, a propane torch, enamel aerosol spray can, a pack of grill lighters, and two pairs of heavy-duty work gloves.

"Which do you prefer?" she asked.

Carson ignored the question. "You think we can get away with carrying this shit around out in the open?"

"Who cares if people see? We have more important things to deal with."

"Unless someone decides to call the cops on us."

"Okay, fine. I'll carry it in my bag. Now which one do you want? Makeshift flamethrower or makeshift torch?"

"Oh God, we're really doing this, aren't we?"

"You keep asking that. I promise the answer will always be yes. Until they're dead or we're dead. Until it's finished, one way or another. Now pick."

"You're intense, you know that?"

"And you're kind of a little bitch, Webber. If you don't pick, I'll pick for you."

Carson frowned. "Fine. I'll take the makeshift torch."

"Good. Then you can carry the broomstick."

Sophia emptied her bag of anything unnecessary, then opened the packages and deposited everything into the bag. She closed the trunk, shouldered the bag, and said, "Any idea where we go now?"

"I thought you said you had a plan?"

"Yeah, that plan ended here, and doesn't pick up again until we find them."

"Well, I don't know. You know more about the legend of these monsters than I do. What did the internet tell you?"

"That they stalk the woods around here, living and hiding out in supposed underground tunnels and caves."

"Right. So, same as the movie. Okay, well, I think I saw a trail map as we pulled in. At the start of a trail at the other end of the parking lot. Start there?"

They walked the length of the parking lot, receiving a few glances thanks to the broomstick Carson carried, but thus far had no interactions with others. At the trailhead, they came to a post with a placard containing a map of the area. They both examined the map for a minute in silence.

"If you were a melon head, where would you hide?" Sophia asked.

"Somewhere where there aren't any trails, probably."

Sophia exhaled noisily. "That leaves a lot of woods to search."

"No kidding. How the hell are we supposed to find where they live?"

"Pick a random spot to venture off the beaten path and hope we get lucky?"

"Lucky. Right." Carson leaned in closer to the map, taking in some of the finer details he glossed over at first. "Hey, here's a thought."

He pointed to a spot on the map directly to the west of Felt Mansion, closer to Lake Michigan, in between two trails that angled northwest and southwest to water, respectively. "We're theoretically looking for under-ground tunnels and caves, right?"

"According to the legend and movie, yes."

"Okay, do you see these squiggly lines through here? These are contour lines."

"Carson, I know how to read a map."

"My bad, my bad. Then maybe you see what I'm getting at. This area here has a significantly higher eleva-tion than where we're at now—which, it even says right here on the map: sloping hills and steep drop-offs. So, what if instead of the tunnels going *down* into the ground, they're more or less level with where we're at now? You know?"

"Dug into the side of the hills, you mean."

"Exactly."

"All right, not bad, Magellan. I say it's worth a shot. That's not all that far away."

They set off down the trail before them. They could follow the established path until about halfway to the lakeshore where it forked. At the fork, they could take a left and go southwest to the lake or take a right to the north along a connector path to another trail that traveled northwest to water. Instead, they planned to forge straight ahead off the trail into the hilly woods.

The first stretch was a little more strenuous than expected. Under the trees everything was carpeted by last year's oak leaves. The trail was mostly clear but sandy, and rose and fell several times in the short distance they had to walk. Carson and Sophia scanned both sides of the trail for any sign of the melon heads, but saw nothing. A part of Carson held onto the lingering fear of the nighttime attacks, but walking the trails now, it was hard to maintain that level of alertness. They passed a handful of other hikers as they walked, and everything seemed so fine and normal.

"Hard to believe this is the place the melon heads supposedly live," he said. "This place seems popular and like it would have people around all the time. You'd think if some demon monsters 'stalked' the woods, we'd have heard more about sightings or attacks or whatnot. You know?"

"I was just thinking the same thing. Although, if our experience so far is any indication, maybe it's true that they're nocturnal. And maybe they only 'hunt' in remote places, where a disappearance wouldn't be linked to this place. If these creatures were smart, and Isaac sure seemed to think they were intelligent, it would make sense that they don't risk being seen. Hell, eliminating sources of exposure are the reason we're even here."

They reached the point where the trail split, and both stopped. Directly before them the ground rose quickly. Though the trees along the hillside were mainly well-spaced and mature oaks, the understory was littered with downed branches and a thick growth of shrubs and other weedy plants. Without speaking, Carson and Sophia seemed to agree to pause for a short time while they pondered their next steps.

"I know it doesn't really matter, but I'm curious," Carson said, breaking the silence. "The narrative in the movie was that the melon heads were the product of an evil doctor experimenting on kids in an insane asylum, right? Do we have any credible reason to doubt that?"

"That is one of the theories from what I saw online. The other theory suggests the melon heads were once human kids with hydrocephalus. There—"

"Hydro what now?"

"Hydrocephalus. Excess fluid around the brain. Big heads."

"Gotcha. Keep going."

"There was supposedly a hospital here with a special ward for these kids. The hospital shut down, and for some reason the kids were 'released' into the woods."

"Okay, a bit farfetched, but on point for an urban legend."

"Yeah, but—"

"Neither of those are true," a raspy voice said behind them.

CHAPTER THIRTEEN

Carson jumped and Sophia emitted a short gasp as they wheeled around to the source.

"Whoa. Easy. I mean you no harm." An elderly man stood about five feet away. White tufts of hair stuck out from under his bright blue mesh trucker's hat that said Wiley's Seed and Feed. He wore a tan jacket despite the mounting warmth, clutched a walking stick in a knobby fist, and all exposed skin was wrinkled as though he'd spent the morning underwater.

"What did you say? Neither were true?" Sophia asked

"I did."

"I'm not sure we know what you're talking about."

"Why, melon heads, of course." He smiled warmly, as only the elderly know how. "I'm sorry, I'm afraid I overheard you two talking about that old urban legend."

Carson exchanged a look with Sophia, unsure what to say.

"Would you like to know the truth?" the man asked.

Sophia laughed, but to Carson's ear it sounded forced. "I don't know what you think you heard, but surely if you're talking about melon heads, the truth is they don't exist."

The old man smiled in a way that made his eyes shimmer. "Very well." He nodded minutely, then turned to continue his walk down the left fork.

"Wait," Carson said after the man had taken a few steps. Sophia elbowed him in the side, but Carson ignored her. The man stopped, looking back at them. "Can we try that again? My name is Carson and this is Sophia. Sorry about that. You spooked us is all."

The man came back to them, a gnarled hand extended. "Arnold, but you can call me Arnie."

They each shook his hand, then Carson said, "Nice to meet you, Arnie."

"Likewise. You folks from around here?"

"We're from the general area, but neither of us live around here anymore."

"Never been here either?"

Carson shook his head and received a nod in return.

"I thought as much."

"Why do you say that?" Sophia asked.

"Oh, nothing nefarious, I promise. You simply have a look about you. Like you're searching for something."

"We're not searching for anything," Sophia said, her voice holding that defensive tone. Carson understood why, had also felt the sense of hesitation, but he wasn't so sure they shouldn't be more receptive to what this guy had to say. What if he really *did* know the truth?

Arnie chuckled. "I don't see many folks gearing up to head off-trail if they aren't in search of something. But, if you say so. Still care to hear what I have to say?" He leaned toward them, a hand to the side of his mouth, and whispered, "You know, just in case you *do* decide to poke around?"

Sophia started to say something, but Carson cut her off. "Sure Arnie, we'd love to hear it."

A family of hikers came by from the north fork, heading down the trail Carson and Sophia had come from. They all waved, nodded their hellos, smiles all around. When they were out of earshot, the old man began.

"Now, you may already know this, but if not, a bit more research would tell you neither an asylum nor hospital ever existed on these grounds, or anywhere in the near vicinity for that matter."

"Oh," Carson said.

"However, in the late '40s, the Felt family sold the estate to a Catholic diocese, turning the mansion into a seminary prep school for boys for more than twenty years."

"Okay, so that would make sense in terms of the myth of the melon head creatures being demon kids with big heads," Sophia said, her eyes wandering a bit in thought.

"Indeed, and it was during that time that the first of the stories and sightings happened. It's also when the phrase 'melon heads' was first used. The locals didn't like the school or the boys attending because they were 'the others.' They came from rich families and, according to the locals, had big egos, or big heads. Thus, melon heads."

"Seriously? That's where it came from?"

"Yes, ma'am. Now, eventually the State bought the Felt Estate, and they—"

"Turned it into a prison! I remember that."

Arnie swung a finger in Sophia's direction. "Exactly right. So, when that happened, there was, quite naturally, a lot of fear and paranoia floating around, which no doubt fed into the stories and rumors that already existed. Parents in that time would have most certainly been telling their kids the melon head stories to scare them into being good little boys and girls, that's all."

"That's all?" Carson asked.

Arnie nodded. "Eventually the State sold it to the Township in the '90s to be used as a public space. It's been restored and used as such ever since."

"Hold on," Sophia said. "*That's* your truth? You just wanted to give us a history lesson to tell us the melon heads aren't real? Wow."

The old man held his pointer finger aloft as if to say *not so fast*. "I never said they weren't real. The melon heads are very much real."

Sophia frowned. "Well, then where did they come from?"

Arnie chuckled. "Can't say for certain. I have a few theories, myself. All rather outlandish, I might add. But that's all they are—silly theories."

"Like what?" Carson asked, knowing if the guy didn't mention the movie then he was probably just another old man looking to spin a yarn.

"Oh, a poor bargain with the devil, perhaps. Or maybe a run-in with a witch in the woods. Something more fitting for the times is an accident involving radioactive material." Arnie shrugged again. "I don't think we'll ever know."

"Huh," Carson said. *No dice*. "Well, thanks for the info."

"How do you know all of this?" Sophia asked abruptly.

"I've seen them."

"You've seen them?" Carson said, suddenly second-guessing everything. Did this guy know about the movie after all? If so, why not mention it? Or did he know something else they didn't know? Did he and Sophia have it all wrong? So many questions, Carson's head started to tickle unpleasantly at the overwhelming thoughts.

"Several times, yes indeed."

"And what, they. . . told you all of this?" Sophia said, clearly still skeptical like Carson had been.

"I've been around a long time. I've seen things."

She shook her head, uttered a barking laugh. "You're messing with us, that it?"

Arnie pressed his right hand to his heart and then lifted his palm to the sky. "Hand to God. I swear I'm telling you the truth, as much of it as I know, at any rate. The melon heads are real, and I've seen them. Multiple times."

Carson exchanged another look with Sophia, his eyebrows poised into a question. She shrugged.

"We have too," Carson conceded.

Arnie smiled lightly. "I thought as much. I am, however, a little curious as to why you two seem intent on finding them now."

Sophia squared herself to Arnie, the toe of her shoe digging into the sandy trail. "To kill them."

"I see. Well, you're not going to find them that way." Arnie tilted his head to the sloping ground behind them.

"How do you know?" Sophia challenged.

"Like I said, I've been coming here a long time. The first time I visited this place I was a man much closer to your age, if you'll believe it. So, that puts it close to four decades, I suppose. Trust me, I know a thing or two."

"Cool. Then maybe you can tell us where we can find them."

"Sophia."

"What, *Carson*? We need to find them to end this."

Arnie spoke before Carson could respond. "I'm afraid I don't know the exact location. I only know you won't find them *here*. I believe they may hide out somewhere near the north end of the park, but it has been many decades since I accidentally stumbled upon their quarters. Besides, even if I did know for certain, I don't know that I could ever live with myself if I sent you off to the creatures and either of you got hurt. Or worse."

The implication hung heavy in the air for a moment before going stale. Without knowing why, Carson got the impression that all three of them fully understood the stakes and were not put off by their mention.

"Okay then. I guess there's nothing else you can do to help us. Let's go, Carson."

Carson's face scrunched. "I'm sorry," he said to Arnie, apologizing for the both of them.

"I'm not," Sophia said.

Arnie, to Carson's surprise, laughed. "I assure you I

take no offense," he said, pausing briefly. "You know, I told myself I wouldn't pry too far into your business, but I'm afraid I am rather curious. Why *do* you have such a desire to find these creatures and put yourself in harm's way?"

Carson thought for sure Sophia would simply walk away leaving the question unanswered, but she stayed put, adjusted her bag on her shoulders, then placed both hands on her hips. She wasn't moving, but she wasn't happy about it, either. Still unsure whether Arnie was telling the truth or not, Carson decided to give a little more, just in case. He said, "I'm not sure you'd believe us if we told you."

Arnie laughed, full-throated. That man was full of humor, it seemed. "Son, have you heard a word I just said? I told you *all* of that and you still don't think I would buy into a bit more craziness?"

"Carson, I don't—"

"We watched a VHS tape. An old, low budget horror movie about the melon heads. Afterwards they attacked us. Middle of the night, miles from here."

The old man whistled. "Fascinating. A tape? I'll be..."

"I knew you wouldn't believe me," Carson said.

"No, you misunderstand. I do believe you. Assuming the film was shot here on location, they feel exposed by you seeing it, is that it?"

Carson hesitated. Sophia had a hand on his arm, tugging lightly, but hard enough for Carson to get her intent. "That's what we figure... but how'd you come to that conclusion so fast?"

"It makes sense, does it not?"

Sophia jumped in. "We've taken up enough of your time. And really, we'd better be on our way. We have business to take care of or we'll never sleep again. Thanks for the info. North end of the park you said, right?"

She nodded to herself without receiving an answer, and with that, she turned, pulling Carson with her. They got a few steps away by the time Carson managed to free himself.

He stopped to look back at Arnie, who had not moved. "If you don't mind me asking. . . why do you still come here? If you've seen the monsters several times, then surely you know what they are and what they're capable of. So why do you come back? Aren't you. . . scared?"

"They are rather frightening little creatures, aren't they? I am not afraid, though," he said, shaking his head. "Not right now, anyway. They only surface at night." He looked to the canopy and the filtered morning sun bleeding through.

"Is that really true?"

"Indeed." His hand twisted repetitiously, digging the end of the walking stick into the soft ground. He and Carson locked eyes for a second, then Arnie took a measured breath. "You know, if you really want to find them—if you really have a death wish—come back when it's dark. Flash your headlights into the woods and you'll see red eyes, glowing among the trees. They'll come to you."

Carson's breath hitched in his throat, caught by the

ominous way the old man had spoken, as if in a spell. Then Sophia spoke, shattering the illusion.

"We don't have any trouble attracting the fuckers. Thanks."

CHAPTER FOURTEEN

C arson followed a half-step behind Sophia along the north trail. She moved quickly but kept looking back over her shoulder. At first Carson thought it was to make sure he was still following along close, then he realized her gaze was going farther back to where they'd left Arnie, as though she were hell-bent on putting distance between the old man and them.

"What's up with you?" he asked.

She didn't answer. Up ahead was a curve in the trail that would take them out of view from the fork in the path behind them. Carson checked back that way one more time and saw Arnie had moved on, continuing with his morning hike.

Carson bumped into Sophia who had suddenly stopped on him. "Hey, what the hell?"

Fully turned around now, she peered back the way they'd come.

"Hello? Earth to Sophia. What are you doing?"

Sophia wheeled on him, an impatient glare meeting

Carson's startled expression. "*I* am going off the trail into the woods right here and doubling back to the area we originally wanted to search. Are *you* going to join me, or would you like to go chase after your buddy and keep chit-chatting?"

"Whoa, hold on. I was not the problem back there. You were the one being a real dick to the guy, although I have no idea why. He told us a lot."

"But was it helpful? No."

Carson scoffed.

"Look," she said, "I'm not going to debate my behavior. I don't trust that guy. Something seemed off. I don't know what, but something. Are you really telling me you didn't feel like that whole conversation was at least a little bit weird?"

He gave her the benefit of at least reconsidering how the conversation went, shifting the broomstick from his right hand to his left. "I don't know. I guess I did wonder if he was telling the truth about any of it."

"Well, it definitely felt wrong to me. Like how he told us we for sure wouldn't find the melon heads hideaway right here, but conveniently forgot where they really were? Just somewhere vaguely in the north?"

"That part seemed pretty innocent to me."

"It seemed like intentional misdirection to me. And, did he look familiar at all to you?"

"What? No. Other than the fact that he looked like your everyday old white guy grandpa."

"Whatever. You don't have to agree with my gut on this, but can we at least agree that we should check this part out while we're here? We still have lots of daylight. We can try to knock this area out, give it a good once over, then move on to the northern part of the park. Does that sound all right?"

Carson gave in. It was solid enough reasoning anyway. "All right, sure. Let's do it."

They slipped between the first line of trees and made their way across the sloping land with Sophia in the lead. Unsure of the most efficient approach to search for the melon head hideout, they opted to head along a straight line toward the lakeshore, move south, then walk back to the trail in another straight line, a process they could repeat until they'd successfully traversed the whole area. Progress was slow, but steady. Much of the ground was thick with slippery dead leaves, brush, or downed limbs, and Sophia, still favoring her bad arm, had to pick and choose their route carefully to avoid large obstructions, all while attempting to maintain a relatively direct path.

Almost two hours passed with no results except exhaustion. They took a break at the top of a bluff, Carson choosing to sit on the sandy ground of the back-dune, while Sophia leaned against a mature cottonwood tree. Trees were sparser up here, giving way to the smaller dune shrubs and grasses, allowing them to catch a magnificent view of Lake Michigan below, its light, teal surface sparkling in the now full, late-morning sun. Low rolling waves pulsed toward the beach, carried by a moderate breeze they could hear in the rattling cotton-wood leaves above.

"It's beautiful up here," Sophia said.

"You know, in all the years I lived with Gran, I never once made it out to Lake Michigan. A real shame in retrospect."

"No kidding? Well, you can make up for lost time now that you're back."

"If we get out of here alive." Carson pulled his knees to his chest and rested his chin in the crook between them.

"You really don't think we can beat these monsters?"

Carson shrugged. "You know me, eternally pessimistic."

"Speaking of pessimistic, I'm not so sure we're going to find the melon heads over here. If you look down there," she pointed to the southwest, "that looks like where the trail comes out to the beach. And if that's the case, there can't be much more ground to search before we hit that other trail. I mean, I'm beginning to wonder if we'll even find them. At this point I'd say we stand as good a chance of finding a cabin and the Book of the Dead as those fucking things."

"Yeah, maybe let's not accidentally summon more demons, please," Carson said wryly, and forced his hand to his lap after realizing his thumb was halfway to his lip. "Perhaps the old guy was telling the truth after all?"

"*Maybe.*"

"I guess we'll find out. Ready?"

"Yep. I'm ready."

Carson stood, brushing the sand from the seat of his pants, and led the way back to the east. Even though the elevation trended downward in this direction, Carson preferred going the other way; without steps or a clear path, there was no graceful way, only awkward lunges down the soft, leaf litter-strewn slope. Reaching a shallow plateau, Carson stopped for a moment to watch Sophia skitter down a particularly steep stretch, ready to offer a hand for balance if needed.

She slipped, loosed an alarmed yip, but then skidded unadventurously on her butt until her feet touched flatter ground and was standing again with ease. "Cake-walk," she said, and laughed, though Carson noticed unease. If she felt anything like he did, the exhaustion had worn her thin, putting her on the cusp of breaking. Then again, she was always the stronger one.

"Watch your step, okay?"

"Thanks, *Dad*. I will."

"Hey, we've got a lot of hiking left to do it seems, and I don't want to have to carry your sorry ass up and down these hills."

"Yeah, yeah, as if you're even strong enough to lift me."

Carson barely heard the insult. His attention was locked elsewhere, and he'd come to a complete stop. A second later Sophia bumped into him.

"Hey, what gives? Move it, Webber."

"Isaac?" Carson whispered.

"Wait, what?"

He felt Sophia grab his shoulder to peer over, but Carson was already on the move, jogging farther down the slope toward his old friend, unmoving under a pile of leaves.

About the same time the illusion his brain had created snapped and he finally realized what he was seeing, Carson's next step met a mat of sticks and leaves that swiftly and easily snapped, sending him careening headlong into the hole beneath. On the way down, he made a last gasp reach for the ground above and caught the decapitated head of Isaac to bring along with him.

CHAPTER FIFTEEN

"Carson? Carson!"

On his back, legs and arms all akimbo, he groaned. Before opening his eyes, he prepared for the worst. His brain sent feelers out along the nerves to his extremities, scanning for pain past the threshold of a normal level. Granted, his entire body hurt, but it was the sting of impact, already fading to a dull ache that may or may not last days but did not mean severe damage.

In the absence of the impact's shock, Carson remembered why he'd fallen.

Isaac. Isaac's *head*. Left eye socket gnawed and empty; teeth exposed through missing chunks of cheek; and gore-matted hair.

"*Ohmygod ohmygod ohmygod,*" he murmured, afraid to peek through his closed lids for fear of somehow finding the head planted on his chest, death's tortured grin greeting him. Of course, he didn't feel the weight of it on his torso and had no intention of groping around for it blindly.

Finally, he opened his eyes. Some light filtered in

from above, but not enough to fully illuminate the dank, dark corners of the tunnel before him. Not enough to expose his dead friend's head, wherever it rolled off to.

"Carson?" Sophia called again, her face hanging out over the opening Carson had fallen through, several feet above, her eyes narrowed against the gloom.

"Yeah, I'm all right," Carson said as he worked his limbs a bit. "I hurt, but I don't think anything's broken."

"What the fuck were you doing? What was that?"

As they spoke, their voices drifted further underground, carrying and dissipating. He listened to its curious transformation as it became replaced by a low, guttural tone from deep within.

He froze. Comprehension hit. Isaac, the hole, this apparent tunnel. *Holy shit, we found it*, he thought.

Carson flung his hand up, desperately trying to shush Sophia.

"What—"

She stopped. Carson pulled his hand back, bringing his pointer finger to his lips, but not daring to take his eyes off the obscured blackness. He planted both hands directly beside himself and lifted his upper body off the tunnel floor, then with incredible care—and still wary of what he might touch or brush up against—crab-walked backwards toward Sophia. When he successfully backed into the wall of dirt he would soon have to scale to get out of the tunnel, Carson's right hand brushed a hard, fist-sized object half-buried in the ground. His heart jumped and stomach tightened, but noticed it was only a rock. He pulled on it, needing *something* to protect himself. It wouldn't come free easily, though, so he left it.

Carson looked up to Sophia's attentive eyes. He whispered, "We have to be *very* quiet, so please don't react loudly. I found Isaac. . . well, his head."

Her mouth dropped open and Carson expected a gasp or blurt of expletives or maybe a shower of vomit, but to her credit she remained silent. She closed her eyes for a moment and shook her head, then came back to him. She mouthed, *Okay, what now?*

He checked down the tunnel again and didn't see or hear anything else, which he took as either a good sign or very bad one. His eyes were adjusting, but he still was not able to make out much of anything, only that the tunnel narrowed quickly. If they intended to go that way —which, Lord help them, he knew Sophia certainly did —then they'd have to crouch significantly. But first, they needed to do something about the dark. . . and Isaac.

He no longer had the broomstick in hand and could not recall losing it. But, from his current viewpoint, it did not appear to be down in the tunnel with him, either. To Sophia, he whispered, "Torch."

Confusion clouded her face momentarily before it clicked. She disappeared, and Carson immediately heard rustling as she MacGyvered the makeshift torch together. He waited as patiently as he could force himself to be, what with the possibility of an untold number of vicious monsters within shouting distance.

Carson tried for the rock again, this time digging his fingers deeper into the dirt around it. With a bit more leverage and a harder pull, it broke free. Out of the ground, it felt lighter in his hand, and longer. He brought it to his face, curious and needing something to occupy his thoughts while Sophia worked. What he saw made him groan.

A bone. A femur from the looks of it, and clearly human, if his knowledge from high school anatomy was still with him.

Carson tossed it aside and stood quickly, his back scraping roughly against the dirt wall. At full height, his head just reached the opening. His view of the tunnel from here was nonexistent, but Carson had to do it, suddenly feeling the sour taste of stale air, the weight of the earth above if it were to collapse—the intense desire to rejoin Sophia on the surface.

He was just able to see her now, the progress she'd made. She had the rags wrapped and secured to one end of the broomstick and was busy soaking them with kerosene. When she finished, she looked toward the hole, jumping slightly at the sight of Carson's head popping out. She quickly regained her composure, though, and came towards him.

"So, they're down there?" she asked, whispering.

"Pretty sure. I thought I heard one growl, but now I wonder if it was... snoring?"

"Weird. How do we want to do this?"

"It's tight down there. I'll have to feed the broomstick in and light it down there."

"Think you can handle it?"

"What choice do I have? We have to go down there, don't we?"

"I think so." She nodded. "Do you want me to go first?"

"No, I will. I'm already down here anyway. Just stay

close behind me and be ready with the blowtorch. Hopefully the tunnel opens up and we'll have room to move side by side. Oh, also, watch your step. There are. . . bones."

She swallowed. "Got it." Sophia passed the broomstick torch down, rag end first, and helped Carson feed it into the tunnel, then handed him a pair of work gloves and one of the grill lighters.

Carson started to bend, but then Sophia said his name. He straightened. "What's up?"

She leaned in, threw both arms around his neck and pulled him into a tight hug. Without letting him go, she spoke directly into his ear. "I missed you. Don't go and die on me."

She let him go.

He offered her a reassuring smile he did not feel, then ducked back under. His eyes were once again unadjusted to the darkness, but he knew as soon as he got the torch lit that wouldn't matter. Carson pulled a glove over his left hand and grasped the broomstick midway, holding the kerosene covered end aloft down the tunnel before him. Holding the lighter next to the rags, he held the catch and clicked the trigger. A puff of flame danced from the end of the narrow metal tube, flickered against the rags and set them ablaze. There was no *whoosh* like gasoline, but even still Carson yanked his hand away from the sudden strong heat, then walked both hands back to the base of the broomstick, keeping the flame aloft several feet away. He stuck the lighter into his back pocket, then shimmied the right glove on.

The light given off by the torch wasn't enormous or

overly illuminating like he expected, but compared to the darkness before, the difference was significant. He could see much more of the tunnel now, but only that it continued for maybe ten or fifteen feet before sliding away to the right. Carson was both frightened and relieved. Thankful to see he was not mere feet from a slew of monsters, yet terrified at the prospect of having to spelunk further underground.

A few feet away to the side of the tunnel was Isaac's head—*Made pretty good distance,* he thought hysterically —but he refused to let his gaze linger.

He gave Sophia a thumbs up, then shuffled deeper to give her room. She came down much more gracefully than Carson, first dangling her legs in, then sliding down in a smooth motion. In one hand she held the blowtorch, in the other, the can of enamel spray. For a moment Carson had an image of her getting antsy and accidentally scorching his back, but quickly shook the image from his head. He looked back once more to quietly warn her about Isaac and not to focus on it, then forced himself to move on. He heard her make a muted sound like a mix between a cry and gagging when she saw it, but then they were past it, on to more immediate and important matters.

There was no comfortable way to proceed. He tried walking mostly straight-legged, bending severely at the waist, but that only served to strain his back. He ultimately settled on crouching and shuffling along, dealing with the burn in his thighs and calves. The torch always leading the way, they followed the tunnel as it curved to the right. Past the curve, the tunnel straightened out and went on for another twenty or so feet where, at first, Carson thought it came to a sudden end. As they inched along closer, though, he noticed the tunnel took a sharp turn to the left. He checked Sophia to see if she saw what lay ahead, and she gave him a nod in acknowledgement.

At the bend, Carson directed the torch around the corner then poked his head around to see what lay ahead.

Even though he half expected it, the sight stopped the breath in his throat. Just beyond the bend, the tunnel opened into a large cavern. At least, Carson assumed it was large. The torch lit up the front part but could not reach the back. Even still, Carson could see as many as ten melon heads. They slept, curled up like dogs in beds of leaves and other ground litter. How many others existed beyond his view, he could only guess. As he watched, Carson marveled at how small and unassuming the creatures looked. Ugly and misshapen no doubt, but without the benefit of gnashing razorblade teeth, glowing eyes, or rabid snarls, the snoozing melon heads looked, remarkably, just like children with big heads.

Admittedly, it gave him pause. But then he remembered the bones. And the carnage. And Isaac. His screams echoed in Carson's ears like the sound of the ocean in a conch shell. The faint, but obvious sound of wet, ripping flesh and snapping of bones like dead tree branches. Carson knew he'd hear all those sounds again if they didn't end this nightmare. Only next time it'd be him and Sophia being shredded into oblivion.

The time was now. Carson inched around the corner,

moving gently into the open cave. Once through the entrance, he moved to the side, leaving room for Sophia to join him, then looked back to check that Sophia was indeed coming.

He gasped. A shadow loomed over her lowered shoulder.

It said: "I'm afraid I can't let you do this."

CHAPTER SIXTEEN

S ophia started, but before she could face the voice behind her, she was sent flying. She careened into the opening, clipping Carson's shoulder and knocking the broomstick torch from his grip. It landed on the dirt floor of the cave with a soft thump, Carson and Sophia following suit.

Carson went sprawling, but Sophia landed with significantly more grace. She hit the ground and rolled, both hands up—still holding their items—and at the ready.

The figure stopped at the opening to the cave, issuing a short, shrill whistle. It planted a walking stick into the dirt at their feet. "I would think twice if I were you."

Arnie.

The cave suddenly filled with a cacophony of low growls, dotted with the occasional snap of teeth and a couple rounds of foghorn-like croaks. Carson didn't need to look behind him to know there were tens of eyes suddenly open and glowing. He ducked his head, bracing for impact...

...That didn't come. But...

"Why?" Carson said.

"Everything is about survival, and I'm *finally* going to be free," Arnie replied matter-of-factly.

The torch continued to burn on the ground, producing an uneven light across the old man's wrinkled and unconcerned face. Carson righted himself, scooting his butt across the ground until he was seated next to Sophia, the handle of the broomstick resting between them.

"I don't get it. Who *are* you?"

The old man stared at him, his eyebrows raised, and mouth set into a frown. "I know I didn't make it obvious, but I'm still surprised you haven't figured it out."

"Jesus. No shit. I told you he looked familiar," Sophia said. "Arnold's your middle name, huh?"

She knew already, but it took Carson another few seconds to make the leap.

"You're. . . no way. Ryan A. Henderson?" he exclaimed, then winced at the loud report of his voice throughout the cave.

"Oh, no need to worry about them. Not yet, anyway. We have a couple things to discuss still. Unless you— Sophia, was it?—don't toss your things aside. Then I should think you'll be dealing with them sooner than later."

Sophia didn't move, and for a second, Carson believed she was going to outright refuse to ditch the blowtorch and spray can. Arnie began a second warning when she finally obeyed. She rolled the blowtorch to her left out of reach and tossed the can after it.

"Good girl," Arnie—or Ryan or whoever—said.

"Fuck you."

Arnie laughed. "You're awfully feisty, aren't you?"

"Why don't you skip the evil villain speech and cut to the chase?"

"Me? The villain?" Arnie said, looking like he'd been slapped. "You have no idea what I've been through, missy. *I'm* one of the first victims. They—" He pointed over their heads, at the melon heads. "—are the villains. The *monsters*. They know it, I know it, and I know *you* know it."

"Then why are you doing this to us?" Carson asked. His voice sounded small and confused and he hated it.

"Because I have to!" Arnie shouted, a wild, animal-like fury welling up in his cheeks and eyes. "Helping them is the only way I can finally be free. I've waited more than thirty years for this, and finally—*finally*—the time has come! You two are the last ones."

"Henderson, my man," Sophia said, her voice a calm and composed manner Carson felt so far removed from. "You're losing me here. Let's reel it in a bit. Did you make a deal with the devil?"

The anger suddenly subsided and Arnie's expression matched Sophia's calm demeanor, along with a chilling resoluteness. "You could say that. They killed all my friends. The rest of the crew?" He shook his head, clearing it of some image dwelling there. "We just wanted to make a silly movie. It was the '80s. Horror was everything and no one gave a shit what kind of product you pushed out. Not yet, anyway. Well, we made the damn thing, but it came bearing gifts." He nodded to the melon heads again.

"How?" Sophia asked. Cool, calm, collected.

"I didn't lie about that part," Arnie said. "I don't know. I didn't know then and still don't know now. It stormed the night we wrapped filming. That's my best guess. I've come to realize there's so much beyond the realm of our normal world. More than we could ever know. I always fancied myself a creator, but I never would have dreamed of something like this."

"Or nightmare," Carson said.

He felt Sophia's hand brush his own, and for a moment he thought her resolve was finally cracking. Then he knew that wasn't the case. His hand wasn't the target, but rather the broom handle adjacent. He forced himself not to look, to give whatever she had planned away, and prayed to a multitude of gods that Arnie didn't see either.

"So, you somehow survived while the rest of the crew died. You still haven't explained why or how. We saw you looked like you'd been attacked on the tape," she said.

"Luck, I guess. My assistant made copies of the tape after things started going crazy. I figured out how many, but not where they went. They got misplaced, sent around, I don't know. But these things, the melon heads, seemed to realize the tapes were a threat. They're smart, you see. And, they came from the movie, so somehow they're connected to it." He locked eyes with Sophia, then Carson, and back again. "I never could explain it, but they're able to find the people who've watched it once the tape has been played. Otherwise, though. . . well, that's where I come in. I said I'd help them. Help them survive, help them find the tapes until they were all gone and they were protected from their existence being exposed."

Carson, desperately trying to keep up to speed, asked, "You can talk to them?"

"I'll spare you the details, but they have ways of communicating."

Sophia forged on. "So, we watched the last copy of the tape, is that it?"

"That's right."

"But we've destroyed that tape!" Carson said in a sudden outburst. "Shouldn't that mean it's over now?"

Arnie eyed Carson with narrowed eyes. "The tape is destroyed?"

"Yes! We smashed it. No one can ever watch it again."

Arnie smiled, letting out a lengthy, relaxed sigh. "Thank you for doing that. Saves me the trouble. But that doesn't matter, not for you two. You've been marked. They want you dead. And once you're dead, my end of the bargain is complete. I'll be free."

"But why not help us kill them? You'd be free that way too," Carson said, fully aware that the monsters could be sinking their rows of teeth into his neck at any second.

"If anything goes wrong, they'll kill me. You can't beat them, and I can't take the risk. I'm sorry it has to be this way, but it does."

There was no remorse or sorrow in Arnie's voice or eyes. Only satisfaction and hunger. "Well, anyway. I suppose that—"

Sophia cut him off with loud, braying laughter that carried on for several seconds before fading to a close.

Then she said, "Remember when I told him not to give us the villain speech, Car? Man, they just can't help it. Old guys really love to talk, don't they?" She sighed, then added quickly, "Duck."

Everything and everyone in the cave seemed to freeze for a full second before Sophia's words clicked.

Carson leaned forward, bending at the waist. At the same time, he felt the heat of the torch as it swooped by, Sophia wheeling it around at Arnie. The old man shrieked and dove to the side, into the cave away from Sophia and the swinging torch.

"Tunnel!" she yelled.

Carson scrambled to all fours and launched himself into the tunnel in front of Sophia. She was on her feet in an instant, spinning to face the monsters, the torch out to ward the monsters off. Carson knew fire killed them, but would it keep them away?

The closest melon heads—four of them—charged. Carson flinched, but Sophia held her ground and the torch firm. The monsters stopped short, giving the flames a wide berth, snarling their displeasure. The cave's darkness and the torch's flickering light had an odd effect on the creatures. The shadows managed to mask the more obvious signs of looking fake—the irony of which was not lost on Carson—and instead enhanced their features. Pale, naked and mutilated bodies covered with veins, purplish and appearing to pop close to the skin. Massive, white heads presenting small, reddish and faintly glowing eyes that watched them, daring them to move. Growls escaped between the snapping rows of dagger teeth.

The melon heads oozed menace and pending torture. For a few more seconds, nothing else happened. Everyone seemed to be figuring out what would happen next. Sophia broke the stalemate first by speaking to Carson. "My bag, Car."

He didn't know what she was getting at, but trusted her instincts over his own. He jumped up and quickly began unzipping the backpack purse over her shoulders. Inside he found an extra enamel spray can alongside a spare propane tank for the blowtorch and an old water bottle with an amber liquid. Carson took a second to wonder just what in the hell Sophia had planned, then grabbed the spray can. He popped the top, readied his finger on the trigger, and found the lighter still intact in his back pocket.

Sophia swung the torch side-to-side, holding the monsters at bay, but that only served to make them angrier, and louder.

Arnie, still on the floor of the cave, screamed, "Get them! What are you waiting for?"

At first Carson thought he was talking to him and Sophia, but he quickly realized Arnie was yelling to the monsters. The melon heads charged again. Sophia swung at them, but this time another one of them leaped into the fray, diving at Sophia from the side away from the torch. Carson saw it all in slow motion—chalk it up to a jet-fueled injection of adrenaline—and leaned back into the cave beside Sophia, simultaneously igniting the lighter and depressing the aerosol can's button.

A short burst of fire exploded at the attacking melon head and, like before in the bathroom at Gran's old house, the monster immediately flashed into brilliant light. Unearthly screeches unleashed into the cave and the melon head became ash.

The rest of the melon heads roared. To Carson, it sounded like a mixture of fierce anger and pained sorrow at their fallen comrade.

Sophia laughed wildly, eyes gleaming. "That's right! Try us, fuckers. We're sending you back to whatever hell you surfaced from!"

Carson caught an object flying towards them out of his peripheral. He shrunk down, but the object was never meant to hit him. The spray can Sophia had tossed aside earlier, chucked from Arnie's right hand, caught her on the forehead. She yelped and stumbled back, the angle at which she fell managing to knock Carson out into the cave, exposed.

Carson backed directly into the wall behind him, hoping to protect at least one side of him from attack. Two of the original charging melon heads converged on him, joined quickly by two more from further back in the cave. He had the lighter lit and the spray can at the ready in no time, but the first melon head was faster.

It dove at his legs. An outstretched, clawed hand snagged his left leg, dropping Carson to a knee. As his cry of pain morphed into one of anger, Carson hit the spray, swooping the sudden blaze of fire from chest level down to the momentarily prone melon head.

The flames only forced the other monsters back but managed to reach the one that had taken runnels of flesh from his calf. The melon head erupted into a flash of fire, the tips of which touched Carson. The heat was intense, shocking, but short-lived; a fresh cry did not have time to leave his throat, and his brain, mercifully, moved right past the moment and onto the next one.

Meanwhile, Sophia had recovered her position and stabbed at the rushing monsters with the broomstick torch. One of her jabs obliterated a monster, but more importantly, bought her a few seconds of time while the remainders slunk back. In that time, Sophia swiped the torch at Arnie again, who had done little to help himself besides staring greedily at them in hopes that they would falter, lose, and be ripped to pieces. Sophia's first swipe at Arnie had missed him before. This time had not. The old man screamed as flames licked his face, scorching his hair. He fell backwards again, writhed on the ground, his hands beating against the heat and the embers.

Carson regained his footing, the searing pain in his left leg threatening to topple him again, but he squeezed the muscle against the agony and held tight, never once halting his sweep with the aerosol flamethrower, driving the creatures back. With a bit more confidence now, he used his gained ground to step toward them and shoot targeted bursts of fire.

One exploded. Two ash. Three, nothing but echoing wails.

Carson pressed the spray can trigger again.

A quick hiss. Nothing. The can was empty.

"Shit! I'm out!"

The melon heads didn't seem to notice right away, but Carson knew he had a few seconds at most. Thankfully, Sophia leaned toward him, swinging the torch in a wide arc around both of them, reestablishing space. "By your feet!"

Carson dropped his gaze to the ground, searching desperately...

There! The enamel spray can Arnie threw at Sophia had landed at his feet. Carson bent, snagging the can, relieved to find the cap already off. He rose—

A melon head landed on him from above as though it had been shot from a cannon, slamming Carson back into the hard-packed cave floor. He screamed as jagged teeth like a hundred tiny knives clamped into the meat of his shoulder below his neck.

Carson had a moment to feel aware that this could be it, the end of him, when Sophia came to his rescue again. She stepped to Carson and dropkicked the ghastly beast in its gigantic head, narrowly missing Carson himself, the toe of her shoe squishing sickeningly into one of the monster's eyes. The thing rocketed off of Carson's back, buying him just enough time to twist, brandish his weapons, and torch the living hell out of it.

Another one down, although Carson had lost count how many that had been. His vision blurred as a new set of melon heads rushed in from the back of the cave to begin their assault, the frenzy and chaos of the situation on the verge of pulling Carson under. He'd done so much, but it was not enough. It was never going to be enough...

"Car, cover me!"

The urgency in Sophia's sudden command pierced the hazy shell forming around Carson's mind. It cleared enough for him to see Sophia on a suicide mission. She leapt into the middle of the cave, shrugging her bag off her shoulders onto the ground, its unzipped compartment flopping open like the loose mouth of a dead fish. She was already turning around by the time the bag came to a rest. Carson noticed a peculiar thing as she fled back to the tunnel: she dropped the torch to the ground alongside it.

His body, working on survival instincts alone, sprang into action, mechanically and methodically torching another incoming melon head while his brain processed the images filtered to it through his eyes.

Sophia's actions seemed less peculiar now, punctuated by her yelling, *"RUN! GO!"*

Carson slipped through into the narrow tunnel, scurrying as fast as his torn leg and wrecked body would take him. Somewhere in the back of his mind Carson registered the old man shrieking again, the repeated issuances of *NO, NO, NO!* acting as staccato notes in the high-pitched howl.

Carson reached the corner, threw himself around it. He spared a final glance back to make sure Sophia was still coming, still going to make it.

She was there, in the tunnel, close. A fierce determination etched into her sweaty, bloody face. Behind her, back in the cavern, Carson saw her bag was alight, and he knew: *any second now.*

But that wasn't all. Motion, in between.

A melon head, launching its small, wiry frame, head first into Sophia's back.

The sound of impact was drowned out by the loudest boom Carson had ever heard, then his world went black.

CHAPTER SEVENTEEN

C arson awoke. All he saw was black, and all he heard was a shrill ringing.

Disoriented. His first conscious breath pulled in smoke, causing the onset of a sudden coughing fit. He hacked the irritation out of his lungs, then pulled his shirt up around his mouth, trying to regather his bearings.

While his body screamed in agony, he pushed himself into a seated position. Then he remembered.

The melon heads. An explosion. *Sophia*.

Had she made it?

"Sophia!" he croaked, his voice dry and raspy from the coughing.

He looked around and finally saw light. He followed it around the corner and was greeted with a fresh wave of smoke. He pulled away, then tried again, lower to the ground.

Up ahead he saw her body, not moving. "Oh my God," he whispered. "Sophia!"

It couldn't be. She couldn't be dead. Not *another*

person he loved. He wasn't even thirty years old, way too young to have lost so much close family. He couldn't handle another. Despite everything they'd been through, the very real possibility of both dying multiple times, he simply couldn't handle losing Sophia too. Not now.

He crawled toward her, calling her name again and again. In the space between attempts he finally heard her groan. He reached her, seeing the back of her shirt was a charred ruin, barely holding together. Carson placed a light hand on her shoulder.

"Sophia?"

"Oh God," she moaned. "Are we still alive?"

The way she said it could not have been more *her* if she tried, and it triggered a relieved bout of laughter that quickly devolved into more coughing.

"Jesus, you sound worse than I feel," she said, pushing up to look at him.

"Yeah, this smoke is killer. We need to get out of here."

"Are there any left?"

Carson had assumed the monsters were all dead since they were no longer being attacked, but he realized now that he couldn't know that for sure. He looked down the tunnel to the cave and watched for a few seconds, then decided looking from that spot wasn't good enough. He padded to the cave's entrance, trying his best to avoid the drifting smoke, and poked his head in. There was no movement other than small fires where the melon head nests had been. He said over his shoulder, "Looks like they're all dead."

"Hell yeah, we did it," she said without an ounce of exuberance. "Let's go."

As they crawled for the exit, Carson found the lighter and spray can. He clicked the lighter on to illuminate the dark tunnel. He said, "I didn't think you'd make it."

"Shit, me neither. I think that last flying bastard saved my life. Must have been a barrier against the explosion before it was incinerated. Ruined my shirt though." She laughed, weakly.

They reached the slight bend that would take them to the exit when they finally realized the problem. There was no light coming from up ahead.

"Nighttime?" Carson asked, confused.

The reality was worse. No exit.

"Oh my God, the explosion must have collapsed part of the tunnel," Sophia said.

"No, that can't be. . . are we trapped here?"

"We can't be," she whined. "We got so far. *We killed the bastards*."

"Maybe there's another way out?"

"Did you see one?" Sophia snapped back.

"No," he said, swallowing thickly. "But we have to check."

"What if we dig out this way?"

"We could," Carson said. "But the tunnel seems way shorter now. Who knows how far we'd have to dig.

Sophia hung her head. "Fine."

They retreated to the cave. The smoke was getting worse, and Carson was having trouble breathing. He knew lack of oxygen was already a big problem, and it was only going to get worse.

In the cave, they stood, needing to move quicker, although Carson's leg forced him to limp. Sophia pointed at what remained of Arnie but did not say anything. She didn't need to. Carson didn't want to look at, or dwell on, the charred corpse for long.

Halfway back, a sound to Carson's left startled him. He swung quickly to the noise, reacting with a quick blast of fire, but there was no monster. Only more falling earth.

Carson laughed uneasily, in spite of everything, embarrassed by the overreaction.

He turned back to Sophia and cried out as a melon head emerged into sight and jumped at them. Sophia saw it and ducked away, while Carson's fingers went to work, hitting the buttons in time to annihilate the monster in midair.

"Damn," he said. "I'm getting sick of that."

"I thought you said they were all dead?"

Carson scratched his forehead with the base of the lighter. "I thought they were. But I think *now* we're good."

They both scanned the area again for good measure but saw no more trace of the melon heads except for little piles of ash.

"What do you think is back there?" Sophia asked, pointing at the back-right corner of the dimly lit cavern.

"Hopefully something good and not another damn melon head."

Carson led the way, makeshift flamethrower at the ready. To his immense relief, there were no more monsters hiding.

Instead, there was another tunnel.

They followed it. And followed it. . . and followed it. Bends, curves, sharp turns. Slow descents and quick rises. They saw it all and walked on for a long time, but eventually the tunnel came to an end. There, before Carson could convince himself that it was a dead end and they were doomed, Sophia got closer and pointed out the tiny bars of golden light stabbing through. She pushed on the barrier and it easily came free. All that stood in the way was a kind of door made from sticks and leaves and other debris.

Sophia and Carson finally emerged from the tunnel, spilling out near a stretch of beach. A shimmering Lake Michigan lay ahead, and the air never tasted so refreshing.

As much as they both wanted to leave this place and never come back, they were more exhausted. Sophia dropped to her butt in the sand, while Carson trudged a little farther, wading into the cold waters, touching Lake Michigan for the first time in his life. It made him cry.

The view was immaculate, and the evening had become one of eerie calm. No matter how hard he tried, Carson couldn't let himself enjoy the peace and beauty, not even for a moment. If anything, it felt like the preamble to yet another bad turn of events. His thoughts returned regularly to the closing scene of *Friday the 13th*, and he had a persistent urge to stare into the woods where they had emerged, certain a melon head was lying in wait to complete the last gasp attack.

But there was nothing. Against all odds, it appeared they had actually won.

They stayed out in the lake for a while, washing the blood and dirt and soot from their bodies, then laid out to dry in the descending sun. Several groups of people strolled by, casting disapproving glances, but no one stopped to help—likely assuming the two were drunk or high or both, never mind the ruined clothes. Even if someone had stopped, Carson and Sophia would have refused help. They made it this far without much of any, and they weren't going to take help now.

When the bottom edge of the sun touched water at the horizon line, Sophia spoke for the first time since escaping the tunnel. "Hey Car, ready to go?"

"Yeah, let's go home," he answered, picking himself up off the ground, his body feeling in shambles. "Well, your dad's home. I need a place to sleep for a while that isn't destroyed."

They followed a group of sunset watchers to a trailhead and back to the parking lot at the foot of Felt Mansion. The trek was tiring, but Carson had already reached a point past exhaustion. He moved on autopilot now.

Twilight morphed into night when they finally reached Sophia's SUV. Sophia found her key fob miraculously still in the small front pocket of her jeans, and they piled in.

As she backed out of the parking space, Carson looked to the woods lining the dirt lot. He promised himself then that he would never return to these woods, no matter what. Sophia rounded the corner of the lot to head out. They had to wait while another car backed out ahead of them, which momentarily broke the beam of light shining into the trees. All a routine occurrence. Except—

Except, as Sophia followed that car out of the parking lot to bring them home, Carson swore he saw a pair of red, glowing orbs about three feet off the ground.

STOP■

ACKNOWLEDGMENTS

I still can't believe this book is real. A thing someone—
You there! Hello!—can hold. Perhaps that's because it
wouldn't exist if it were solely up to me. In which case,
some thanks are in order.

First, to Korie. Your support in this silly endeavor
means the world to me. Where would I be without you?

To my parents. The OG first readers. You made me
this way. I hope you're happy.

Much love to my sisters, friends, and other family
who've been so enthusiastic and supportive. It's hard to
express just how important that encouragement is
to me.

To Alexis, for convincing me to send that email. And
everything else.

Enormous thanks to Alan Lastufka for making this
dream a reality. I'm astounded by your tireless efforts to
make this book a sight to behold. I can (and do) sleep
well knowing you put so much time and energy into
making it look so dang cool. I won the indie pub lottery
when you agreed to publish my little monsters. And to

the rest of the team: Nancy LaFever and Erin Foster, for shaping and sharpening this story into its best form.

Thank you, to Marc Vuletich, for absolutely *nailing* this cover art. The melon heads are perfect, and I find myself staring at your work often. I feel confident that your art alone will sell some copies.

Finally, to all you readers. Whether this is your first experience with my work (I'm sorry?) or you've come back for more (I'm *so* sorry), you give me life. I write because I have to, but I get such a thrill when y'all take a chance on me. Thank you.

ABOUT THE AUTHOR

Alex Ebenstein is a lifelong Michigander, where he lives with his wife, son, and dog. His daytime mapmaking career supports his nighttime addiction of writing horror and other dark speculative fiction. He is the author of *Curse Corvus*, as well as the founder and owner of Dread Stone Press, an independent small horror press. Connect with him on social media @AlexEbenstein and keep up with writing news at alexebenstein.com.

A NOTE FROM SHORTWAVE

Thank you for reading the first Killer VHS Series book! If you enjoyed *Melon Head Mayhem*, please consider writing a review. Reviews help readers find more titles they may enjoy, and that helps us continue to publish titles like this.

For more Shortwave titles, visit us online...

OUR WEBSITE

shortwavepublishing.com

SOCIAL MEDIA

@ShortwaveBooks

EMAIL US

contact@shortwavepublishing.com

STAY TUNED FOR
THE NEXT BOOK IN THE
KILLER VHS SERIES

BRIAN McAULEY

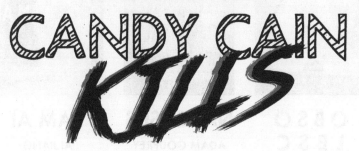

CHRISTMAS COMES EARLY
NOVEMBER 2023

SHORTWAVEPUBLISHING.COM/KILLERVHS

ALSO AVAILABLE FROM SHORTWAVE PUBLISHING

ALSO AVAILABLE FROM SHORTWAVE PUBLISHING

ALSO AVAILABLE
FROM
SHORTWAVE PUBLISHING

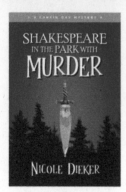

Milton Keynes UK
Ingram Content Group UK Ltd.
UKHW042355070923
428218UK00004B/59